JOHNNY FAIRWAY!

LETS KEEP KEEP DRINKS

& OF HOLES

LOTS PLAY!

P

REAL
AMERICANS

BEST REGARDS
MY FRIEND!

VITO

OCT
2019

REAL
AMERICANS
Don't Tread On Me

Vito Anthony

XP BOOKS

Xulon Press
2301 Lucien Way #415
Maitland, FL 32751
407.339.4217
www.xulonpress.com

XP
BOOKS

Printed in the United States of America.

LCCN: 2019909766

ISBN-13: 978-1-5456-6830-6

CHAPTER ONE

VITTORIO PAPAVESE FELT THE SOLID STONE OF THE Vietnam Veteran's Memorial beneath his hand and the heavy weight that the endless stretch of names placed on his chest. V-man, as his friends called him, was in his middle sixties and still pretty fit from years of competitive soccer and growing up on the East Side of Detroit. When he was a kid, the sport recognized at the time was boxing, where he competed in the Golden Gloves, fighting against a wide mix of other kids from all over the city. His once-dark hair had started turning grey, but his age hadn't dulled his sharp perception. Even while mourning the loss of fellow soldiers, he was aware of the little girl holding her father's hand while skipping down the path to his right and the older gentleman approaching on his left, leaning heavily on a cane. His vision was as clear as a bald eagle, his tenacity was that of a trained Doberman, and he could be as deadly as a bamboo viper. He was a no-nonsense guy deeply dedicated to his country. The oath he took so long ago, at nineteen years old, still stood today: to defend this country, anytime, anywhere, from all enemies, foreign or domestic.

He had spent the bulk of the day working with amputee patients. For the past fifteen years, he visited the veterans at the Walter Reed National Military Medical Center in Bethesda, Maryland, at least three times a year and had come to know them pretty well. In his time with them, he learned the emotional trauma that was unique to soldiers who lost limbs in combat. He made it a personal goal to do whatever he could to make their reintegration back into society after active duty even if just a little bit smoother. He had raised over $2,000,000 in various charity events and sponsored over twenty-five medical service dogs, in addition to building a barrier-free home for a double amputee veteran from his area. The culmination of the trips ended with a Christmas party in December for all the patients and their families. The clinic was decorated to kick off the Christmas season, and everyone looked forward to the event.

During each trip down to DC to meet with the wounded veterans, he stopped at The Wall and the Statue of the Nurses to reconnect with the 58000-plus men and women who gave the ultimate sacrifice. He would never forget them. In his mind, he had always wondered what happened to the commitment of the generation before his, remembering FDR's famous December 8, 1941, speech: "The American People in their righteous might will win out to absolute victory." They won. What about us? Did we win? It was a war Kennedy started, Johnson, didn't know what to do with, and Nixon ended. It was the most intense war we ever fought. We killed over 1,000,000 North Vietnamese soldiers, and averaged over 250 days per year of combat, for over ten years, almost triple that of WWII. There were no parades, no special thanks from the public or the politicians, but what it did create was group of bonded Americans, veterans, dedicated to serve and defend. To the V-man, this was enough. He knew what they had done and didn't need a slap on the back and a phony smile by the ungrateful who would never know or understand the price that was paid and the pain that many continue to deal with.

"V-man." A familiar voice came from the steady stream of tourists passing by the monument.

V-man looked up to find Jay walking toward him with his standard lanky gait. Even at sixty years of age, the tall, sandy-haired, blue-eyed, squeaky-clean guy hadn't lost the youthful all-American look about him that he had on day one of combat. They hadn't been friends right away. People gravitated toward Jay with his open friendliness while they were put off by V-man's standoffish demeanor.

They embraced in a half hug, half handshake before finding their way to a bench on the grassy area adjacent to the memorial. They both sat in silence, taking in the gravity of the memorial. Each silently said a prayer for those who had given their lives for the war. The warm April breeze rustled through V-man's hair as the sun warmed his back.

A smirk came to Jay's face, breaking the solemnity of the moment as he looked at his buddy. "Hey V, what did you say that tattoo stood for again?" he said, nodding toward the tattoo on V-man's arm. It depicted a winding snake with an American flag and the words "Don't Tread on Me."

V-man shook his head. Jay had asked the same question countless times and was only asking it again in an effort to rib him. "What kind of American are you that you don't know what that means?" he shot back with his usual retort. V-man had always been a serious guy, and Jay knew it.

Jay, on the other hand, hadn't been affected by his childhood growing up in the rough side of DC and his unfortunate luck as a teenager that had ended his dreams of being a professional basketball star.

To hear him tell it, Jay was set to be the next Larry Bird. As a rising star in his high school, he was already being scouted by colleges, but one too many knee surgeries took him out of the game permanently, shortly before he was drafted for Vietnam. He never let go of the passion, transforming it into a career as a basketball coach in the same DC area high school that he had graduated from.

V-man shook his head, thinking about when they had first met. From the moment he was drafted back in early 1966, at only eighteen years old, he had one goal: fighting for his country and keeping his unit safe. He and Jay were both in the 227 Airmobile Assault Helicopter Battalion of the First Air Cavalry. Vietnam was a new kind of war without a defined battlefront. The unfamiliar terrain made ground vehicle movements nearly impossible and entirely impractical. The helicopter battalions played a huge part in the movement of troops, re-supplying, and air cover, forcing the men to learn as they went where a mistake could cost them their lives. Even when the guys did everything right, the choppers didn't have long shelf lives. Manning the air assault meant they were the most vulnerable to enemy fire. V-man didn't do anything half-assed, so he was the first in line to volunteer for the position of door gunner, giving him a significantly shortened life expectancy, even for the helicopter assault team.

On an emergency resupply mission, Jay's chopper took heavy enemy fire as they rose up above the canopy cover after dropping off supplies. They had only made it two or three klicks beyond the drop point before the bullets ripped through the hydraulics, sending the chopper spiraling toward the open grass field below them. V-man watched from behind the gun of his own chopper as the black smoke billowed from the tail end of the copter, and it started losing control.

"They're going down!" he shouted to his pilot. "We gotta go back." V-man didn't even consider the danger. As soon as he suspected the fate of the other crew, he knew they were going back. Time was of the essence during extractions, and they didn't have time to mess around with indecision. His own chopper took a sharp turn in the sky as the

4

wind pulled at his green fatigues and gravity threatened to pull him out of his seat behind the M-60 machine gun. As Jay's chopper came back into sight, all hell broke loose. The entrenched enemy opened fire. V-man handled his machine gun like an extension of his own body, raining a hail of bullets on the enemy that could have come from five gunners rather than one.

Jay's copter was lying in a crumpled heap in a field. Crashing in the open made for better odds of surviving the crash but left them vulnerable to enemy attack. The Vietcong would have watched them go down the same as V-man and his crew had. They would be working on moving in to finish the job and salvage any leftover artillery and ammo they could.

V-man threw off his harness and leapt from the chopper as it hovered close to the ground. Running low, he approached the copter that had skidded to a stop on its right side, tearing up the grass and mud as it went. The landing skids jutted out at an odd angle toward the sky. V-man climbed the side and pulled the door clear off. The heavy smoke made it hard to see.

"Hey? Anyone, can you hear me?" he called into the opening he had made.

Low grumblings were the only response. V-man crawled deeper inside. To his left, the unconscious pilot hung to the side where his harness kept him fastened to the inverted seat. Beside him, another pilot struggled with his straps, trying to free himself. In front of V, he saw Jay pinned beneath the machine gun. V pulled the gun aside and grabbed Jay by his fatigue jacket and hauled all hundred eighty pounds of him out of the helicopter. With one arm around him, V half-carried and half-dragged him to the waiting chopper, passing more guys going in to rescue the remaining crew.

Ducking low, they climbed on board the helicopter that took off as soon as the rest of the men were on board, to evade a fury of bullets whizzing past. V-man climbed back into his gunner seat and, half standing and half sitting, commenced firing. As Jay lay there on the chopper floor, he watched as the V-man, who was deadly with that mounted M-60, was returning fire in blazing fashion. Somehow he had supplied all tracer rounds in his ammo box and was spraying any and all enemy positions. As Jay watched and admired this guy's grit, he thought he detected a slight grin on the V-man's face. *Oh shit*, he thought, *this fucking guy likes it*!

As the craft flew low through the dark night, the voice of the pilot, Sky King, came through the intercom. Sky King was a nickname given to him by the V-man, taken from a popular TV show in the sixties because of his outstanding abilities in the cockpit of a chopper. A graduate of West Point and a dedicated Army pilot, King was the only guy V-man wanted to fly with. Anyone who flew on his crew had to be elite. They volunteered for all missions anytime, anywhere. They always said he was so good he could land the helicopter in your garage.

"Got a few damaged fuel cells and took some dead hits, but I can get us back to forward command," Sky King's voice came through the crackling headphones. The news was a relief. Landing anywhere but the base command in the central highlands would have probably meant their deaths.

Once they landed at forward command, Jay was transferred to the field hospital. In the hospital, the message in the expressions of the rescued team was clear: *You saved my ass, brother, and I'll be there for you.*

Up until the rescue, V-man had known each guy in the 227th but hadn't made any friends. He had a natural tendency to keep to himself and gave off an air of seriousness that he had learned from his strict

Italian upbringing back in Detroit in the '50s and '60s. The guys mostly left him alone, assuming he wouldn't be much fun to hang around with. The rescue changed that.

Jay spent a few days in recovery, healing up from a fresh gash in his already-bad knees. The day he was released from the base camp infirmary, he found V-man meticulously cleaning his specially adapted M-60 7.62 caliber machine gun with dual handles. V-man spent some part of every day with a brush, standing beside the chopper, making his gun shine. He took on the cleaning, maintenance, and resupplying of the chopper as his personal duty. His guns, always in top condition, never jammed.

Jay hadn't known V too well. Most guys thought he might be kind of a smart-ass, but that smart-ass had never looked as good as he did at midnight in the middle of nowhere, as they appeared over the treetops flying low with a faint light of a moon that in another thirty minutes would have closed any opportunity for that extraction.

Jay had never been a man of many words, but as he approached V-man, he managed, "I owe you one," in his thick Maryland accent.

Without looking up from his work cleaning the barrel of the gun, V-man had said with his usual mild sarcasm, "Well that's what we are here for. Just part of my job."

Jay shook his head with a smirk. He knew the wild kick-ass kid would be his friend forever. He wondered how a five feet, seven-inch, 150-pound kid got in so much shit and always came out alive. He learned through time that growing up on the East Side of Detroit with strict Italian parents had given V-man an education in hard work and gratitude. V's dad had worked in the Eastern Market packing houses, getting paid piecemeal. It was a tough way to make a living, but they made it work.

Now, sitting on the bench, looking at the names of all the lives lost in Vietnam, V-man felt lucky to be alive with his good buddy.

"You know, it wasn't all bad. Growing up in the sixties, we had it pretty good with our hot cars, hot chicks, and good music," V-man said into the silence. He started humming his favorite tune, "The Way You Do the Things You Do," before breaking out in the lyrics, "You got a smile so bright; you know you could have been a candle."

The song brought a smile to the lips of both men. During their youth, Motown was just breaking onto the music scene in a big way, creating a musical renaissance.

"How about "Help me, Rhonda?" Jay asked, as he sang a few lines.

"Man, what is the matter with you?" V-man asked. "Don't ruin my good mood with your washed-out shit. You know better."

Jay laughed out loud at how easy it was to rib V-man.

"Listen, I got a letter from Ron out in New Mexico. They are trying to put together a Vietnam reunion with some of the guys," He got Tommy B from Chicago and maybe some of those big mountain guys from Montana and Colorado," V-man said. Jay lifted his eyebrows skeptically. "You gotta help me get some of the guys together. Come back to Detroit with me, and we can see if we can make this happen. I think I know where to find Valenzuela."

Jay suspected that there might be an underlying ulterior motive in V-man's crazy head, but he was always up for one of his adventures, so he shrugged and said, "Well, I can't let you have all the fun by yourself. I'm in."

Chapter Two

Anastasia hurriedly unzipped her camou-
flage jacket and pulled open the heavy barn doors, giving a quick smile
to the buck head with massive antlers hanging on the far end. She double-checked the safety of her 30–30 lever action Henry rifle before
placing it carefully on the rack beside the others already lined up along
the wall. She had been out since the predawn light in the deer stand,
hunting, but family dinners at the Kazenko household were sacred, and
she didn't want to be late, so she slid the door closed again and hurried
across the driveway to the house. She stomped the mud off her boots
before unlacing them and carrying them into the house.

"Here comes the hot shit! Thinks she can be late because of she is
going to be starting her new job tomorrow," her brother, Ivan, called
from the dining room table. She hurriedly sat down, after giving a punch
to his shoulder. He grabbed his wound in mock agony. Luckily, their
mother was still in the kitchen, putting the final touches on the traditional Russian meal, so she didn't notice Anna's late arrival.

"Ivan, don't give your sister a hard time. We are all very proud of you.
My little girl has grown up," her father, Oleksandr, said, standing back
and smiling fondly at his daughter, who the family always claimed was
his favorite one. He grabbed her sideways into a big bear hug. When

she was a chubby little baby, she had practically lived in his arms. Since becoming adult, her baby fat had melted away to reveal a slim, athletic, beautiful blonde, but that didn't stop her father from hugging her whenever he got a chance. She enjoyed the embraces and knew that in his heart she would always be his little baby girl.

"You are stepping into some pretty big responsibility over there on the bridge. Let's hope you can step up," Pavlo, Anna's other brother, said.

"Well, I don't put much faith in your opinion since you were so wrong on our first hunting trip," Anna said with a sly smile.

She was considerably younger than her brothers. Everyone in the family suspected her arrival had come as a shock to her parents, but that didn't stop her father from adoring her. Since the time she was born, her brothers had been going out deer hunting. From the time she was big enough to hold a rifle, her father had quietly taught her about gun safety, taking care of a gun, and of course shooting. When it finally came time to take Anna, her brothers set her up in the worst position, laughing the whole time about how she wouldn't be able to hit anything. Not only did she manage to make a kill, but it ended up being a bigger buck than either of the boys had ever taken down. With a gleeful smile, she had presented her prize to her father as both of her brothers stood beside her with arms folded across their chest in defeat. Her father beamed with pride as he insisted it get hung on the wall of the barn for everyone to see. The brothers saw it as a challenge, and the friendly family competition never ended.

She knew that Pavlo's teasing was all in fun, but she never passed up an opportunity to give him a hard time about her impressive first kill, which as it turned out, also remained the family record. She had to admit she felt some trepidation about the first day on the job.

"Tomorrow is a very important day. You are working for your country," Oleksandr said with a beaming smile on his face. "Your country is counting on you. Although it may not seem that way right now, your job is essential to the protection of this wonderful country that has welcomed us with open arms. You will be the only thing standing between our country and the potential danger that tries to infiltrate our borders."

"I know, Dad," she said with a patient smile. She did recognize the importance of her new job and had spent her time hunting that day, trying to recognize some of the growing anxiety she felt for her first day as a border patrol agent for Homeland Security.

Growing up, she hadn't necessarily pictured herself as a member of Homeland Security. Although she was first-generation American, her parents had instilled a deep pride and devotion to the American way of life. They had been the benefactors of the American dream shortly after they had arrived in the 1950s. Her father was born in the Ukraine while her mother had lived in Russia. Oleksandr recognized the unjust oppression and dangerous dictatorship of the Iron Curtain and worked with his father in the Underground, gathering radio intelligence in an effort to help shift the balance of power. Her parents met by happenstance and fell in love, which was a dangerous affair at the time, with prejudice between Russians and Ukrainians running high. After falling in love with Anna's mother, Tatyana, Oleksandr was no longer satisfied living in the dangerous conditions and fighting against the impossible authoritarian rule. After marrying in a secret ceremony attended only by Oleksandr's parents, he convinced Tatyana to escape with him. They paid every penny of their savings to get passports and traveled to America, where they settled in a small farming community outside of Saint Clair in the thumb area of Michigan. They came to America filled with an optimistic hope and a strong work ethic. Olek answered an ad for a laborer for an older couple who needed extra hands on the dairy farm. He brought Tatyana along for the interview, and the older couple, who had no kids, treated them like family from the moment they met. After getting the job, they lived in a small, two-bedroom bunk house on the farm, which they fixed up over time, making it their own. They worked from 3:30 a.m. every morning, proving their dedication until they worked up to more responsibility on the farm, overseeing other workers. Learning about the culture, they integrated into the local community. When the couple who owned the farm retired, they wanted no one but the Kazenkos to have it. When the Kazenkos bought it, they poured their heart and souls into the operation.

They held onto their Russian and Ukrainian traditions, but by the time Anna was born, her brothers had fully assimilated into American life, and her parents had become well-known staples in the community. The farm was the first priority for the entire family, with everyone pitching in every morning, after school, on weekends, and in the summer. It became the foundation of their value system. When she was not on the farm and didn't have a rifle in her hands, practicing her shooting with tin cans lined up along the fence, Anna sought out sports. Her tall, lean body seemed perfectly designed to excel at volleyball, earning her scholarship offers to top universities around the country. When she presented the opportunities to her parents, they were of course delighted in her success, but she saw a sadness hidden beneath the revelry. It reflected her own misgivings about spending so much time so far away. She didn't want to give up her passions and her dreams, but she knew she had to stay close to home. After writing her regrets, turning down the scholarships, she accepted admission into a local division three state college. She continued playing volleyball with great success, winning championships while studying criminal justice.

When she first enrolled in the program, she didn't have a definitive vision of her future job, but she had grown up listening to her father's stories from the Ukrainian Underground, working to overthrow the corrupt government. His experiences working on radio espionage filled her with excitement and an underlying need to always fight for justice. She felt fiercely protective of America. Their life here saved her parents and provided her and her brothers with endless opportunities that they would not have known back in Russia. Every night, when her father tucked her into bed, he would tell her stories of the Ukraine and the Iron Curtain. Not all of them were bad. She learned about her grandparents, and how they made the best borscht, a staple of Russian cuisine containing beets and cabbage, meats, potatoes, and herbs. He told about how his mother would knit by the fire on cold winter evenings and tell him stories. He also told stories about his espionage work that sounded like fantastic adventures to her young mind. She would fantasize about being in the Ukraine and fighting with the Resistance or collecting data with her father like some super-spy from a James Bond film.

Criminal justice became her opportunity to live out those dreams in real life. As her education developed, she decided that Homeland Security would keep her close to home and give her an opportunity to use her criminal justice background for good. She graduated at the top of her class before going into the GL-5 training program, where she excelled again, specializing in both weapons training and hand-to-hand combat, surprising all of the large men who found themselves bested by a tough blonde girl. The job offers came quickly after her graduation, and she jumped at the chance to work with border control on the Blue Water Bridge, spanning from Canada to the United States.

Tatyana walked through the open archway from the kitchen into the modest dining room. They lived in the original farmhouse, which hadn't been updated much, aside from the furnishings and decorations. She placed a steaming pot on the table and served out a thick beef stew into each bowl.

"Are you ready for your first day tomorrow?" Tatyana asked Anna.

"Not much to be ready for, Mom," Ivan said between spoonfuls, "She is just a glorified traffic cop."

"Very funny," Anna retorted. "Oh, you just think you are smart because you put on a suit every day and shop out our products."

Ivan had spent most of his youth working on the farm until he saw an opportunity to promote their dairy to local grocery stores. He found considerable success, making a name for the farm at most of the chains throughout Michigan.

"All work is valuable work," their father said in his calm lecturing tone. Ivan and Anna shared an amused look at the familiar phrase they had heard during their entire lives.

"Is your uniform pressed?" Tatyana asked. She always thought of the practical necessities that acted as the glue holding the family together.

"I have it hanging in my closet," Anna replied.

"We should go out afterward to celebrate," Pavlo said. "Jimmy and Buddy are coming by tomorrow night. Jimmy just bought a new Remington Model 700 30–06 bolt action hunting rifle with a new Leupold VX 3–9x40 Riflescope. They are going to zero it in tomorrow night. I am sure you would be interested in giving it a try."

Anna's face lit up at the thought. They all recognized that she could probably zero it in quicker than all the other guys combined, although they would never admit it out loud. Jimmy and Buddy were both farm kids like Ivan and Pavlo. They had gone to school together and spent most of their free time hunting and fishing together.

"Okay; meet you here after work," she said.

"Sounds good," Pavlo said.

The dinner progressed in the same way it always did. They each gave updates about their lives, ribbing each other where they could get a good joke in, while their father doled out sage-like advice that they had all heard before. When the meal finished, Oleksandr pushed back from the table, rubbing his ever-growing stomach that pushed out over his belt.

"Another delicious meal, my sweet," he said, leaning over to kiss Tatyana. Even after all their years of marriage, they hadn't lost that spark of true love. "I am going to work in my office."

"You know, Dad, one day we are going to find out what is in your office," Pavlo said, smiling.

"Now that Anna is a big hotshot for Border Patrol and Homeland Security, we are going to have her spy on you," Ivan said.

Oleksandr laughed his full-throated laugh before turning to go. "You may not like what you find," he said ominously. For as long as Anna could remember, her father had spent countless hours alone behind the locked door of his office, a closed off room within the barn. From the outside, it looked to be about the size of a single-car garage. It had no windows, and their father remained very tight-lipped about what was inside, despite years of begging. As a young girl, her imagination ran wild, trying to think up possibilities for what was behind that door.

One time, she had gathered enough courage to follow him outside under the cover of darkness. Once he was inside his office, she crouched down beside the outer wall of the barn office with the leaves and mud brushing the edge of her nightgown. She pressed her ear up against the red shingles of the barn. Sounds of muffled men's voices met her ear, traveling through the thick walls. After only a moment of intense listening, she felt a hand on her shoulder and nearly jumped out of her skin.

She looked up at her father, who instead of looking at her with angry reproach, wore a warm smile. "You will have to get better at reconnaissance than that, little girl. Now back to bed," he said, picking her up and carrying her back into the house while humming a traditional Ukrainian lullaby.

Anna took his words as a challenge and never gave up. Although she never managed to set foot inside, she had come to the conclusion that her father used the office as a base station for radio surveillance. What he was following and why, she couldn't venture a guess.

CHAPTER THREE

V-MAN PUSHED THE DOOR OPEN, ALLOWING STRAY sunlight into the dimly lit bar. A few patrons looked up to see who had come in before refocusing their attention on their meals. From first impressions, the bar looked like any other hole-in-the-wall, local dive found on any street corner in any big city. The outside didn't display any signage to indicate what stood behind the thick brown wooden door. Inside a long, well-worn bar took up the right side from wall to wall. A smattering of round tables with plastic, red-and-white checkered tablecloths filled the rest of the space. At the odd in-between hours, only a few regulars sat at the bar nursing beers and eating late lunches or early dinners, depending on their own schedules. Despite its lackluster appearance, it felt like home to V-man. Familiar 1960s Motown, made famous in Detroit, played through the bar, mixing with the news on the TV.

"Hey, Hun," the rough, vaguely feminine voice of Brenda McBride greeted him. It carried a hint of an Irish accent held over from her parents who had arrived from Ireland when her mom was still pregnant with Brenda, without a penny in their pockets. It hadn't been an easy life, and Brenda had done a lot of hard living in her prime.

One day, when the bar was in its infant stages after the change in management, in desperate need of job, Brenda waltzed into the door like she owned the place, picking up dirty dishes, wiping tables down, and telling the owners what to do. Big Mike, AC, and V-man just shrugged their shoulders and gave her the job. Since then, she became the mother figure of the group, keeping them all on the up and up.

The place never looked so good. Brenda made it "Army clean."

"Afternoon, Brenda," V-man said. "You met my good friend Jay yet?" He motioned to the tall man standing behind him in the doorway.

"Nice to meetcha. What are you havin'?" Brenda asked, moving behind the bar and pulling down two glasses.

"I will have an IPA lager," Jay said.

Brenda and V-man shared a look before breaking out in laughter.

"Honey, I think you are in the wrong place," she said through fits of giggles. "We got Pabst Blue Ribbon or Stroh's, none of that flower, hipster shit that passes for beer nowadays."

"I guess I will take Stroh's," he said.

"A Stroh's for me, Brenda," V-man said, still shaking his head over Jay's choice in beer. He made his way to the well-worn leather-topped stool at the end of the bar that had become his unspoken reserved seat. On any day he could be seen sitting there with his iPad listening to George C. Scott quoting General George Patton, FDR in his famous speech to Congress after the attack on Pearl Harbor, JFK, and others. None of the patrons at the bar would ever dare sit in it for fear of being permanently removed from the premises. Above him, the flat-screen TV hung on the wall, the only new piece of equipment in the whole place, running local and national news programs most of the day. And don't come there to watch an NFL game—that was not going to happen. "I have left you alone with those DC education elites too long, Jay. Good thing I came to rescue you when I did."

"Hey, what can I say?" Jay said, shrugging.

Brenda slid their beers down the bar. The door to the back kitchen swung open, and a huge mountain of a man walked through.

"Look who's back in town. Who's this?" Abel Cane said as he leaned against the bar beside Jay. AC had a powerful presence that at six feet, five inches and 245 pounds couldn't be ignored. His dark skin and well-toned muscles, which hadn't deflated despite his age, helped with the tough-guy persona. "Haven't seen you in here before."

"AC, this is my buddy Jay from DC. We served in the 227 Assault Helicopter Battalion with the First Cav," V-Man said.

The scowl on AC's face transformed into a welcoming smile as he reached out and slapped Jay on the back with more force that he intended, bringing a low grunt from Jay. "A fellow Army man, eh? Always welcome here—welcome home, brother," AC said.

"Sure am," Jay said. His East Coast, DC accent made him stick out surrounded by Detroit natives.

"What brings you to the Corner Bar?" AC asked.

Jay lifted his beer to his lips with one hand and pointed his thumb toward V-man with the other. AC nodded slowly in understanding.

"What new crusade are you on now?" AC asked.

"Better to fight for something than live for nothing," V-man said, quoting General George Patton. No one bothered asking where V-man had gotten the saying. "I am trying to get some guys together for a reunion. Jay's the first one I enlisted."

"Are my pigs in a blanket ready yet?" The interruption came from an equally large man walking through the front door. The question didn't match the thick Polish accent, but AC's down south signature dish was

Big Mike Babinski's favorite food. He threw himself into the stool beside Jay. He lifted his chin toward Jay, silently asking the question, *Who is this new guy?* V-man made the introductions as Brenda delivered his food.

"This place have a menu? I could use some food, too," Jay said, looking around.

"Nope, no menu," Big Mike said around mouthfuls of food. "We got three things for lunch and dinner, pigs in a blanket, V-man's famous meatball subs and . . ."

"All right, I will take a meatball sub," Jay said with a shrug.

AC leaned into the kitchen and shouted, "Need a meatball out here."

"So, were you planning on starting?" Jay asked.

"I have a few ideas about where Valenzuela might be," V-man said.

"Man, if Valenzuela wanted to be found, he would have been," AC said.

"We're family. Always will be. Not going let him miss the reunion," V-man said.

AC understood exactly what V-man meant. They had been in Vietnam together. AC had grown up in the neighborhood of Detroit right next to V-man's. When the draft swept through and claimed half of V-man's graduating class, AC was drafted right along with them. They hadn't known each other before they both walked into the induction center in Fort Wayne, Michigan. There was a mix of fear and excitement that filled the room as they moved through the process, each kid searching for familiar faces. As V-man waited for his turn with the doctor for his mandatory physical, the elbow of his neighbor kept finding its way over the arm of the chair and landing between his ribs.

"You need an extra chair?" V-man asked.

There was sense of uncertainty, about a room full of eighteen-year-olds who knew they might be shipped off to their death, facing an enemy 12,000 miles from home, who was entrenched in their jungle surroundings.

"Nah man, just need a bigger one," the kid said.

They both broke into laughter and became inseparable, both by choice and by circumstance. From the induction center, they found each other at Fort Knox, Kentucky, for basic training. After that, they transferred on to Advanced Infantry, jungle-oriented training in Fort Gordon, Georgia. It was a new type of combat training that the Army had designed on the fly as they struggled to adapt to the jungle guerrilla warfare of Vietnam. After infantry, they volunteered together at the Special Airborne Jump School in Fort Benning, Georgia. Those recruits had to learn how to jump out of airplanes even if their fate only led them to be foot soldiers.

There was a special bond between them as two kids from the same area of Detroit, traveling to a country they never thought they'd be able to see. With the chaos of an endless stream of unfamiliar faces moving around them constantly, they found solidarity in their common experiences from a childhood on the rough city streets.

They got separated when V-man volunteered for helicopter battalion, and AC was assigned to infantry. It was assumed that V-man wouldn't come back. The common mythology was that gunners in the helicopter battalion had a short life expectancy. Almost 12,000 helicopters flew in the Vietnam War, logging over 1,000,000 hours of flight time. Almost have of them were lost, killing over 5,000 pilots and crew members.

After the war, when V-man showed up at AC's door, he could have knocked AC over with a feather. He stood on his mother's porch in the summer heat, shaking his head in disbelief. Despite their need to keep up a macho persona, they hugged each other tightly.

"Shit, man, I can't believe my eyes," AC had said.

"You thought I would let you be the only one to come home and be a war hero?" V-man asked.

Neither one of them was the same kid who had flown out of Georgia Army Training bases, but they reconnected and never lost touch again. V-man went on to start a successful real estate company, while the bar fell into AC's lap by happenstance.

After the war, AC bounced around from one job to the next, living with his mom and his little sister. About seventeen years after coming home from Vietnam, all hell broke loose at home. His mother and sister were in the midst of a massive all-out fight over an unplanned pregnancy. AC had been raised by his deeply religious mother, praying before every meal and going to church every Sunday. His sister's pregnancy out of wedlock flew in the face of everything his mom held sacred. Before the pregnancy, his sister had ventured out on her own, opening a restaurant and bar that had reached mild success. On her own, struggling to raise a child and run a business, she spent her weekends partying to burn off the stress. The occasional party drug turned into a daily habit that she depended on to get through the day. The bar fell into disrepair. AC did his best to support her, trying to convince her to get help.

One night his phone rang, displaying his sister's number. When he answered, the only noise coming from the other end sounded like labored breathing.

"Hello?" AC asked. He has just gotten home from his day job, stocking shelves. He had an hour to grab something to eat and get changed before he had to clock in at the night club to stand watch as the bouncer at the door. He listened to her breath come in ragged gasps as he felt a sinking feeling in his stomach. "Chloe? You there? What's going on? Is Jerome okay?"

"AC, help." Her voice sounded like it came from far away.

"I am coming, Chloe," he shouted into the phone as he pulled his coat on and ran for the door.

Waiting for the bus on the corner of his apartment complex, with the rain drizzling on his head, felt like an eternity. Without a car, he had no choice but to wait for public transportation. When the bus finally pulled into her neighborhood, AC still had a few blocks to go before he made it to her front door. His feet pounded the uneven pavement as he pushed passed the gangs of teenagers hanging out on the corners. Her apartment building finally came into sight as he puffed in and out, trying to catch his breath. He took the steps two at a time and punched in the security code. He threw the thick metal door open, busting into the dingy hallway that led to his sister's front door, past graffiti-covered walls. He put his hand on her doorknob and hesitated to take the final step. He had a sinking feeling that he knew exactly what he was going to find behind the door.

He found her lying in bed, struggling for air. The discarded remnants of her night's fun sat on the nightstand behind her. Her skin had lost all of the warmth that made the men turn their heads to get a second look. Her face was gaunt with a sick, gray quality. AC wondered when he had last paid her a visit and feeling guilty that it had been so long. A frantic pressure developed in his chest as he debated calling for an ambulance, putting her at risk for jail time.

"AC," she whispered. He rushed to her side and picked up her hand, which was already turning cold. He leaned in close to hear her scratchy and fading words. "You have to take care of Jerome. You are all he has left."

AC felt hot tears trail down his face and started shaking his head violently against his sister's words. "No, Chloe. I am going to call for help."

"Please, AC. Listen." She opened her eyes and held his gaze with an intensity that brooked no argument. "Take care of Jerome. He needs you. Take the bar. Use it to make a life for you and Jerome. Please."

"Chloe, Jerome needs you." He picked up his phone and dialed 911. Having her alive and in jail was better than not having her at all.

By the time he heard the sirens wailing down the street, she was limp and cold in his arms. As they wheeled her away, Police Captain Forest Williamson walked through solemnly, sparing an unfriendly glance toward AC.

"You taking the kid?" he asked.

AC nodded yes.

When he needed him, V-man showed up, no questions asked. He stood by his side through the funeral as AC struggled to comfort the eight-year-old boy who clung to his hand, staring with wide, empty eyes. AC had no experience being a father figure or a business owner, but he moved himself and Jerome into the apartment above the bar/restaurant and set about fixing it up to see if he could pull a profit. V-man introduced AC to Big Mike. Big Mike grew up in Hamtramck, a small city within the city of Detroit that was settled by Polish immigrants in the early 1900s. It had earned the nicknames, "Hamtown" or "Poletown" because of its heritage. V-man had met Big Mike on leave from Vietnam. He was a bouncer and worked the door at one of the toughest and hottest bars on the eastside, The Falcon Showbar. V-man was fond of the place and spent many nights there, trying to make up for lost time. V-man had seen Mike in action, an absolute destroyer with a punch that would knock guys out on their feet. The big man liked the action, and it seemed to have increased since the V-man shows up. They became friends. They went to a blind pig one night after the bar closed and gambled and drank all night and left with most of the money. They then ended up eating homemade stuffed cabbages and Polish sausage at his aunt's restaurant at 6:00 a.m. They were street guys and enjoyed each other's company. They were the brother to each other that neither one had.

When AC and Big Mike stood side by side, they looked like the same guy duplicated in black and white. The similarities didn't stop at their looks, either. Both were well-known forces in the neighborhood as guys that no one wanted to mess with. They were both the star football players of their high schools before using their strength and formidable talents and appearance to gain employment as strong arms and bouncers.

They hadn't known each other long before V-man put them in touch. V-man couldn't have explained what exactly inspired him to tell AC about Big Mike; he just had an instinct that the pair were exactly what the bar needed. He was right.

So, AC understood the power of Army buddies who were more than friends; they were friends who were brothers. There wouldn't be any talking V-man out of finding his brothers. He simply nodded and knew that they were at the beginning of something.

The door opened again as a young boy in his late teens entered the bar, pulling a trolley stacked with boxes behind him. He shook his head to move the shaggy mop of blonde hair out of his blue eyes. Homer Purvis was originally from Tennessee but moved here with his military dad who was transferred to Selfridge Air National Guard base twenty-five miles north of the city. His dad was killed in an aircraft accident and left Homer on his own. He saw the group sitting at the bar and altered his original route to meet them there.

"I've got the delivery." His voice had a slight southern accent.

"Homer, you know I don't start working until I have finished my meal," Big Mike said, grabbing the kid into a rough hug.

Homer smiled. "I just need you to sign a piece of paper, Big Mike."

"Not until I am done. Have a seat. Someone grab another serving of pigs in a blanket," Mike called to no one in particular.

"That's okay, I have other deliveries to make."

"Nonsense," Big Mike said, pulling Homer down into the bar stool beside him. Mike and Homer had bonded together in a father-son relationship. Mike never married and had no children, and with Homer's dad deceased, they were good for each other. Big Mike was very protective of Homer, and a few months back when Homer had come in the bar all upset as he explained to Big Mike he could not get that new truck he was supposed to pick up that day. The dealer had raised the price of the new truck and quoted him less on the trade-in value of his old truck. He had done odd jobs at the bar to earn extra money and had saved to get this special Limited Addition 4x4 pickup. Big Mike was not happy and glanced over at V-man. V-man saw that angry look and knew immediately what needed to be done. Big Mike gave V-man the paper work and had Homer drive the three of them to pay the dealership a visit. Upon arriving, Big Mike and Homer parked directly in front of the dealership main entry and got out and stood by the old truck staring directly into the showroom floor. V-man went inside with the paperwork. In fifteen minutes, after V-man met with the salesman, then the sales manager, and finally the general manager, and in all the conversations, referring to and pointing at Homer and Big Mike, walked out and reported the good news. Not only did they reduce the price $1500.00 from the original deal, they threw in a three-year, bumper-to-bumper warranty and a $100.00 gas card. Homer was elated as they drove back to the Corner Bar in his new 4x4 triple black Ford F-150 Extended Cab Raptor. He asked V-man how he got that deal. It was easy. I told them that big guy out there is going to either drive away in the new truck, or he was going to drive the old truck into the showroom without opening the doors! The three of them had laughed all the way back to the bar. V-man noticed the special bond between the two of them.

Brenda walked to the swinging kitchen door and called back, "One more pigs in a blanket. Jerome, can you bring it out?"

Whatever response Jerome may have made didn't travel through the door. Homer's dad had died in Desert Storm, leaving him to take care of his mom and sister. He got a job delivering meat for the local butcher. When he showed up at the bar one day to try to encourage AC and Big Mike to switch their delivery service, Big Mike agreed without hesitation, finding an instant connection with the boy. They only ever ordered ground beef and sausages, but they ended up being Homer's biggest customer.

"Pigs in a blanket ready," Jerome yelled through the swinging door.

"Bring it on in," AC shouted back.

Jerome pushed through the door. There was a family resemblance between AC and Jerome. He was tall with sharp eyes that, in a few years, with the wrong kinds of influences, could become dangerous. His muscles hadn't developed yet the same way AC's had, but he wasn't someone to mess with.

"Who's it for?" he asked. His voice always sounded slightly angry, as if he carried around some hidden angst for the world that only he could see.

"Homer," AC said, nodding his head toward the boy.

A dark look passed between the two boys as Jerome dropped the plate in front of Homer when it was still an inch or two off the table. The clatter resounded off the walls as the food threatened to spill from the plate. The two boys didn't like each other but really didn't know why. Exposure to old prejudices in their early years had stayed with both of them.

"Boy, you gotta be more careful," AC thundered, but Jerome had already walked back into the kitchen. AC shook his head. He felt more and more exasperated with each year that Jerome grew older.

"Have you seen this shit?" Jay asked tapping V-man on the shoulder and directing his attention to the TV.

V-man picked up the remote and turned up the volume, drowning out the noise of music and talking around them. The news anchor stood outside of the Detroit federal courthouse.

"The so-called 'underwear bomber' has been in prison since his attempted terrorist attack aboard a Northwest Airlines flight almost eleven months ago. He is due to stand trial here in the upcoming days. We expect heavy protests."

"I don't know why they don't just fry him," Big Mike said, moving over to sit by his side. "Don't waste time with a trial."

The V-man looked at Big Mike but said nothing. He also was thinking of just that punishment, and a slight grin came over his face.

CHAPTER FOUR

ANNA STIFLED A YAWN BEHIND HER HAND, LOOKING around to make sure no one saw her. The excitement of the first day on the job had started wearing off somewhere around the two-hundredth car. She was stationed on the Port Huron, Michigan, Sarnia Ontario Blue Water Bridge, a congested, well-traveled nexus between Canada and the United States. During the day, the sun reflected off the clear blue water that gave the bridge its name, creating a serene and peaceful backdrop for the countless traffic that moved through the area. When the sun sank below the horizon, the lights on the bridge glowed with life, making the water turn a deep solid black.

Once over the bridge and into the States, cars were directed to booths set up similar to old-fashioned toll booths. Each of the thirteen lanes was directed to a small kiosk where a border patrol agent would check the drivers' papers and ask them questions. Every once in a while, a car might get flagged, or on even rarer occasions searched, but for the most part, the job became routine and monotonous as the cars and the passengers who rode in them blurred together.

Anna stood within her booth in her deep green uniform with a golden Border Patrol badge on her breast pocket. She huddled down in the patrol-issued coat as the cool evening wind blew in off the water.

Her booth provided little protection from the elements, and she tried to keep her mind off what it would be like in the dead of winter with the snow piling up around her. For the time being, the weather was turning warmer with the spring.

Every time she slumped with boredom, her eyes traced the horizon where the sky met the water, and she felt an enormous pride that she was essentially the gatekeeper, protecting her country by screening and preventing would-be troublemakers from entering. Not everyone was lucky enough to be put on active duty during their first day on the job. Her high test scores and efficiency with firearms led her to the prestigious posting.

She shook her head to refocus her attention as the next car pulled up. A hand stretched out of the small red Toyota with passports. Anna peered into the car at the small family of three. The passports were US-issued, indicating they were citizens.

She ran through the typical questions. "Where are you traveling from?"

"We were visiting family in Ontario," the man behind the wheel replied.

"How long were you staying there?"

"Just the week."

"What did you bring back?"

"My son brought back a stuffed animal souvenir."

Anna nodded her head and reentered the booth. It was entirely routine. She scanned the passport before handing it back and waving them along. The next car that pulled up was a black Honda SUV. Sometimes noting the make and model of each car was the only difference between each stop. This one was different in other ways, too, though. As the man

31

behind the wheel came into view, Anna saw that he had light brown skin and a dark hair, placing him as a Middle Easterner.

"Good evening," he said with a thick accent.

Anna smiled as she took his papers. She felt a hesitancy that she hadn't experienced with any of the other travelers. It was all too easy, she realized quickly, to jump to conclusions based on someone's looks, accent, or country of origin. It would be a dangerous habit to adopt if she didn't censor herself quickly. She nodded her head and ran through her usual questions, reminding herself that everyone had a right to the American dream like her family did, as long as they were willing to do their part and adapt.

"What brings you to the US?" she asked.

"I am here for some hunting,"

"Oh," Anna immediately perked up. "I am a hunter myself. Where are you looking to hunt?"

"We go to upstate Michigan." The man in the car, named Rahim, according to his passport, didn't seem interested in swapping hunting stories. Upstate Michigan and the Upper Peninsula were well-known areas for deer hunting. Just this day alone, she had countless people respond with the same answer.

"What do you do in Canada?" she asked.

"I am a computer programmer with NCIX," he replied.

Anna nodded. She had an uneasy feeling growing in the pit of her stomach, but she couldn't put her finger on what was causing it. She chided herself again for letting prejudice get in the way of doing her job, but her father had always told her to trust her instinct.

"You hunting alone?" Anna asked.

"No, I am meeting some friends up there," he replied impatiently.

"That's good, not always safe to hunt in unfamiliar woods alone. How long do you plan on staying in the United States?" she said, bringing the questioning back to standard protocol.

"Only the week."

"When was the last time you were in the country?"

"Last year."

His abruptness sounded rude, especially since it was a standard question. "How long have you been living in Canada?"

"Does it matter?" he asked.

Anna looked up, meeting his eyes. He stared back at her with a firm resolve. "Sir, these are pretty standard questions and shouldn't be difficult to answer."

"I have lived here for five years," he said grudgingly.

"Is this your first time deer hunting?" She wasn't sure what had prompted her to ask the question, but the answer surprised her nonetheless.

"No, we do this every fall," he said. "And I never get questioned like this."

Anna eyed him. She itched to defend herself, but thought better of it, imagining that a defense would only make her look weak in his eyes. Without any more questions, she turned back to her booth to look at the papers he had handed her. Everything about them looked legitimate. She scanned the passport without any flags coming up. She double-checked the number on the hunting license to make sure it wasn't expired and then did a cursory search of his name in the database without any results. She sighed before reluctantly turning back to him. She tried to tell herself that she would deal with endless streams of cranky, condescending jerks in her new job. She counseled herself to grow a thicker skin and get over it, as her brothers would probably say.

Despite her self-talk, she couldn't get rid of the unsettling thought that kept itching at the back of her mind. Something didn't feel right, but she couldn't figure out what.

She handed him back his paperwork and waved him along. As she watched his car drive past the checkpoint, she looked up with a sudden realization. She figured out what was so strange about the man and his story. Without checking with her superior, she typed the license plate into the system and flagged it for suspicious activity with a pounding heartbeat. She finished her shift with an unsettled, antsy feeling, like her nerves were coursing with electricity.

When her shift finally ended, she made her way through the department headquarters until she came upon one of her superiors, sipping coffee in the break area with a few other agents. Her superior had his feet up on the table and was telling a story about some guy he had apprehended with a trunk full of drugs. The guys around him laughed at the idiocy of the perpetrator, not even trying to disguise the drugs.

"Excuse me, Mr. Clark?" Anna said when the noise of laughter died down. The eyes of all four men turned to her. Everyone had treated her very nicely since she had gotten the job, but there was a certain sense of hierarchy that underlined every interaction. The veteran agents, while helpful and kind, felt like the new agents should have to prove themselves to get the same respect they gave each other. It was the same mentality with her hunting crew. Until you proved your skill, they assumed you didn't have any.

"How was your first day, Anna? Everything go okay?" Mr. Clark asked.

"Yes, sir. Thank you for asking. I wanted to talk to you about one car I flagged," she said.

"You flagged a car?" one of the other agents said.

His tone made her momentarily question her decision. She had never had a problem speaking up. Living with two big brothers and their friends, she had plenty of experience standing up for herself. She took a breath and reminded herself that she belonged here, and it was her job to flag suspicious people.

"Yes, I did," she said firmly, looking the agent directly in the eyes, daring him to challenge her. He didn't say anything else.

"Why did you flag a car?" Mr. Clark asked, pulling up the log for the night.

"His paperwork all checked out, and I was about to let him go, but he kept talking about hunting. He said that he was an experienced hunter and he went up every fall, but something seemed off to me from the moment he pulled up. He was wearing all of his hunting gear in the car." She said this as if it explained everything, but she was met with puzzled gazes.

"So?" Mr. Clark asked with his gruff, no-nonsense voice.

"So? You don't wear all of your hunting gear when traveling five minutes down the road, let alone if you are in the car for hours. He had on his Carhart jacket, which is way too hot and bulky for driving. Any experienced hunter would know that."

Mr. Clark shared a look with the other guys in the room. "Anna, I am glad that you are being diligent, but that isn't a lot to go on. We will keep the flag on his car, but beyond that, wearing strange clothes isn't something we can do much about."

Anna felt the same frustration that was a constant companion when dealing with her brothers. She respected Mr. Clark's authority and even his more experienced judgment, but she knew something wasn't right.

Mr. Clark watched her stew before speaking, "Anna, you are an asset to our team. Your test scores and your performance in training set you apart from just about everyone, but you are new. It takes time to get a feel for how everything works." He smiled and placed a reassuring hand on her shoulder. "Try to just take it one step at a time." There was a sense of dismissive finality in his words.

Anna nodded her head respectfully, "Thank you, Mr. Clark."

She stepped out of the room and headed for her locker. He was right. It was her first day on the job. Was she reading into the guy's strange behavior too much? Was she trying too hard to prove herself?

Anna shook her head to try to clear her thoughts. She pulled open her locker and gathered her personal things before finding her car and driving home.

The driveway to the family farm house was packed tightly with her brother's trucks and the two trucks of their friends. Anna pulled to a stop in the only available spot before going inside and getting changed out of her uniform into her typical blue jeans and T-shirt. As she stepped outside, she grabbed a hoody to wear. The weather had been unseasonably warm for November, but as the sun went down, the wind picked, up creating a chill.

She found her brothers and their two longtime friends in the shooting field. For as long as she could remember, they had a dedicated field for practicing their shots with targets at the far end and tables set up for the guns. Her father had roped off the field for safety, but they had long since disintegrated from the elements. Everyone on the farm just knew that it was the shooting range, and they had to use common sense and not go walking through the field during target practice.

Buddy and Jimmy could have been her long-lost brothers. Although in appearance they all had different features, their interests, behaviors, and even body language looked exactly the same as her brothers. They both grew up on farms, while deer hunting in their free time. Now they stood with their backs to her, huddled around the table ogling their new weapon. The highly rated Remington with its stainless steel barrel and newly mounted scope was a thing of beauty! They were all anxious to see and hear it perform. A few months before, she did the same with Buddy's new Limited Edition LWRC AR-15 with Trijicon scope, all in a camo finish. He had broken somewhat with tradition, but the new AR was extremely accurate and exciting to rapid fire with its thirty-round mag.

"Step aside, boys, and let the real hunter have a look," Anna said, as she stepped up beside them.

"One day on the job and the power has already gone to her head," Ivan said with a smile, as he ruffled the hair on the top of her head like she was still a little kid. His words struck a sore spot after her conversation with Mr. Clark, overshadowing her excitement for the impressive weapon laid out in front of her.

"You okay, Anna?" Pavlo said, noticing the slump in her shoulders.

"Yeah, normally a new gun like this would have you doing backflips to show off," Ivan said.

Anna smiled. "I am good. Here, give me the rifle." Her fingers moved quickly as she adeptly readjusted the scope before bracing her elbows on the table and leaning in to look through. In three quick shots, the scope was zeroed. She picked it up, clicked on the safety and passed it back to Jimmy, who whistled with admiration.

"There it is," Ivan said with pride.

A smile spread on her lips as her confidence came back in a wave. There was a reason she had been hired for the border patrol and a reason she was placed at the checkpoints for her first day. She wouldn't be able to do the job if she second guessed her natural instincts every time someone didn't see what she saw. At that moment, she made the decision to follow her gut.

Chapter Five

V-MAN STEPPED OUT OF HIS BLACK SUV IN MEXICAN
Town, a corner of Southwest Detroit off I-94 West, claimed by residents
of Mexican heritage when immigrants started settling there in the 1940s.
After crossing onto Bagley, the streets came alive with culture. A massive
influx had arrived in the '60s, '70s, and '80s, contributing to an over-
haul of the neighborhood. The locals took a lot of pride in their culture,
taking the opportunity to clean up and rid the area of the crime it had
been known for. Street justice prevailed as the law of the land for anyone
who lived there.

As V-man and Jay walked the street, large, brightly colored murals
covered the brick façades of local stores. A large church dominated the
street, with a billboard announcing Sunday service in Spanish and other
community-oriented events. V-man stopped in front of a food truck,
advertising the city's best enchiladas and tacos.

"What are you doing, man?" Jay asked.

"I'm becoming part of the community" V-man said, as if it were
obvious. They watched the bustling movement of the locals while they
waited. They felt suspicious eyes look them up and down as they stood
out among the mostly Hispanic population. With food in hand, V-man
led the way into a local grocery store with a Mexican flag flying beside the

American one. The bell jangled above the door as they stepped through. The shelves were lined with foreign products labeled in Spanish. V-man approached the man who lounged against the counter, his attention captivated by something on his phone.

"Was wondering if you could direct me to Morrell Street?" V-man asked.

"You walk a block up and then have to go onto Morrell. What you going to on Morrell?" he asked, finally looking at V-man, pulling his attention from whatever had distracted him on his phone.

"I am looking for my friend, Ramon Valenzuela. I have it on pretty good authority that he lives down there," V-man responded.

The guy's mouth compressed into a thin line as he considered V-man's words. Obvious outsiders, they were treated with common courtesy but weren't privy to any inside information about anyone from the 'hood.

"Don't know who you are talking about," he said.

V-man nodded and took his cue to leave. He had confidence in the skills he gained working in the real estate profession for over forty years, to find any house he might set his mind to finding, and growing up on the East Side, he understood the ways of the street. As they made the turn onto Morrell, V-man felt a gentle tap on his arm as Jay caught his attention.

"We've got company," he whispered, lifting his eyes to indicate a group of four men behind them.

"I noticed. The store clerk must have called ahead to the welcoming committee."

"You sure this is a good idea?" Jay asked.

"Don't go soft on me, Jay. We are finding "LaBamba." The nickname V-man had given his friend. He had the same last name as the famous rock singer of the '50s.

40

"Why didn't we just drive over here?" Jay asked.

"You don't go into a neighborhood like this unannounced. It's street culture and respect. We wouldn't get one block without it," V-man answered.

Like Jay, V-man had met Ramon Valenzuela when they were deployed to the same company and battalion in Vietnam. On any given night, LaBamba could be found cooking up some delicacy by the open fire of the base camp. The guys crowded around to get first dibs on the meal. He did the best he could with the Army-issued provisions, but he had a way of bartering with the Air Force to get some extra ingredients that the Army never got, to spice up the food. He had lost both legs in a mortar attack, pulling guard one night. The only thing that saved him from bleeding out were the two tourniquets put on by guys in the next foxhole, a little Italian kid from Detroit and a basketball guy from DC.

V-man and Ramon were tight while serving in Vietnam; they were similar in size and stature, shared the same ethnic values, and would argue who was the best ever professional boxer, pound for pound. With Ramon calling "The Fists of Stone" Roberto Duran the best, and V-man countering with "The Brockton Blockbuster" Rocky Marciano, the only undefeated heavyweight of all time. But ever since the emergency evacuation chopper lifted him out, he had stayed away from any of his Army buddies, although not many of them were left. He closed up as a bitter resentment settled over him for being confined to a wheelchair. Back then, they didn't have the technology available in the present or the understanding of prosthetics and PTSD to provide him the real help he needed. Coming back from Vietnam, soldiers were met with harsh criticism that should have been leveled at politicians and were left to suffer silently and rebuild their lives independently.

V-man was there in Mexican Town, hell-bent on making contact with his friend for the reunion. All of his previous attempts at reconnecting had failed. He hoped that bringing Jay to town would change his luck.

He had purposely parked in front of the store, putting a strong obligation on the owner to watch out for V-man's triple black GMC SUV with dark windows. It was street culture and was understood by all. Visitors were given respect as long as they didn't break the rules.

V-man and Jay continued down the block, passing rows of brick-fronted townhomes with well-manicured lawns that still held the same cultural flavor of the main stretch of Mexican Town, with flags and lawn decorations. Their new entourage followed at a distance but didn't even try to hide their intent of keeping an eye on the newcomers. They were younger than V-man and Jay by at least forty years. Some of them could have passed for high school kids, with their pants sagging low and baseball caps turned off to the side.

"Hey, man, you lost?" one of the older guys shouted from his position in the middle of the street. His voice held a thick Mexican accent with street slang.

"Not looking for any trouble. Just visiting," Jay shouted back.

This elicited laughter from the group, "Only people who are trouble say they aren't looking for trouble," the kid called back.

"I know where we are going. So, don't worry about it," V-man said sarcastically. He didn't want to provoke them, but he wasn't someone who could stand by while others pushed him around. The porches had started filling up with people, hoping to catch sight of the afternoon matinee or whatever action was about to go down. Jay shifted his eyes warily toward V-man. This was the exact kind of situation that V-man might make worse by throwing gas on the fire. Jay thought back to the night of the rescue. *If I see him with that fucking grin, shit!*

They turned the corner as the group continued to throw jeers and questions in their direction. A few houses in, V-man slowed to a stop. The thin driveway was dominated by a full-sized black van with handicap stickers. If he hadn't been sure before, seeing the van bolstered his confidence. The guys who had trailed behind filed into the yard and took casual postures within Jay and V-man's line of sight. Not trying to outwardly intimidate, but making sure they were well aware of the watching eyes, V-man tipped his head back to look up at the house. All of the windows were tightly shuttered. It looked dark and unoccupied. The yard was well maintained, and V-man was careful to stay on the brick path that led to the front door. He didn't get very far before the front door swung open and another Hispanic guy stepped out onto the front porch. Taking long strides, he stopped V-man in his tracks on the walkway, as the other four guys moved to surround him.

"You know what you are doing there, man?" one of them called.

V-man simply nodded. The guy blocking his path looked V-man up and down, with suspicion written all over his face, before steeling his gaze to meet V-man's eyes with a harsh, intimidating stare. If V-man had to guess, he would place him in his mid-twenties, but he wasn't always great at guessing ages. V-man held his gaze, waiting for an introduction. A minute passed as the silence stretched between them, neither one willing to break the eye contact.

"I'm looking for an old friend. A Vietnam buddy of mine," V-man said into the silence, when he got tired of waiting. "A Ramon Valenzuela. You know him?"

"No man, nobody like that here."

"I am Vittorio. What's your name?" V-man asked, reaching out his hand as a friendly gesture of introduction.

"Gomez," he replied without inflection, ignoring V-man's outstretched hand and turning to go.

"You sure?" V-man called to his back. "I got good info that he lives here." Out of the corner of his eye, he saw movement in the front bay windows as the thick cream-colored curtain shifted ever so slightly.

Gomez turned back to look at V-man again. "I think you have overstayed your welcome, old man," he said with a sneer and condescending glance.

V-man nodded and gave a quick smile as he started turning to leave. "Thanks for your time. We were just looking for our friend. We've got a reunion coming up and wanted him to be part of it."

"Like I said, I don't know any Ramon Valenzuela" he said with a disparaging smile. Gomez shared an amused look with his buddies as they celebrated scaring off the old guy. V-man watched the look pass around the group, as a thorough stillness settled over his body. He let the subtle laughter die before he moved with an unexpected speed no one thought an older man would be capable of. He swung around until he stood only inches from the Gomez's face. His blue eyes cold as steel held a wild, dangerous edge as Gomez's mouth hung open in surprise and he reflectively stumbled backward.

In a near whisper, spoken in Spanish, that forced the entire group to strain their ears, V-man said, "I said, he is a friend of ours, and we will find him." His piercing eyes stayed trained on Gomez as he struggled to recover from the shock and embarrassment of being bested by an old man they had so severely underestimated. As Gomez nodded almost imperceptibly, V-man pivoted on his heels and walked off the property without another word. There were no more smiles passing between the guys behind him. V-man guessed he wouldn't be invited to the next Cinco de Mayo block party, but he wasn't much of a fan of Mexican music anyway, so he shrugged it off. When he reached the street, he spared one last glance at the shades of the house in time to watch them rustle again, as if someone had been watching from inside.

Gomez looked around for an outlet for his frustration. He ripped a branch off a nearby tree before turning on his friends and waving them away with a heated gesture. "Nothing else to see." He turned on his heels and stalked into the house, closing the door behind him with a reverberating slam.

"Gomez." The voice came from the dark living room off to the left of the entryway. Gomez turned to see his Uncle Ramon positioned beside the window in his wheelchair.

"Who the hell was that asshole? Was he really a friend of yours?" Gomez asked. "'Cause if he wasn't, I would have the guys beat his ass for trying to show me up like that."

Roman raised a hand to quiet his nephew. "We were brothers in another life."

"He is damn lucky I let him walk away without teaching him a lesson," Gomez shouted.

A rare smile darted across Ramon's lips before it disappeared without a trace. "Maybe you are the lucky one. I wouldn't be so sure. That is a very serious man out there. Don't let your arrogance blind you to what is right in front of you." He turned his attention back to the small sliver of light coming from the opening in the shades. Gomez started to go before Ramon spoke again. "Follow them. I want to know what they are up to. Make sure they don't see you."

"Whatever you want, Uncle," Gomez said, nodding before going through the front door to gather his gang and follow V-man.

Chapter Six

Anna stood at her booth, checking paper-
work, asking her questions and waving cars by. She tried to keep her
attention where it belonged, but she found her mind wandering to
the suspicious car from a few nights ago. Much like her brothers, her
co-workers had ribbed her endlessly about what they saw as her over-
enthusiastic reaction of tagging a car whose paperwork all checked out.

"Hey, Anastasia, you catch any real criminals yet?" they jeered when
she entered the break room the next morning.

"Be careful, Anna, we get a lot of knitters coming through the border,
too. Better check their needles are in order!"

"Don't worry, I will just check them against the ones you keep in
your locker, Cody," Anna retorted, unfazed by the doubt. A day or two
ago, she might have let it get to her, but now it just added fuel to the
fire of her innate drive to prove them all wrong.

As the next car rolled slowly through the checkpoint, Anna pulled
up the license plate that she had flagged the other day. The system, in
her opinion, was outdated and not adequate in monitoring potential
suspects. Rather than keeping a constant log of the plates' locations,
it was only updated if an officer happened to run the plates for traffic
violations. She knew that Homeland Security had requested a national

license plate registry tracking system that would allow for data from any plate-scanning device that came in contact with cars to be compiled, but as far as she knew, that was a slow-moving process that might not see the light of day in her lifetime. That meant that unless Rahim was careless, she wouldn't ever know his whereabouts. All she had to go on was his word that he was heading up north for hunting. As she absent-mindedly checked the paperwork of the next car in line, she kept an eye on the slow-moving multicolored circle that indicated her computer was processing her request.

She knew that if she ever found Rahim, she would have to figure out a way to keep better tabs on him. During her education, she had taken as many surveillance classes as she could. At the time, most of her classmates and even a few professors had encouraged her to pursue more useful or relevant skills. They collectively felt that surveillance would be irrelevant to a border patrol agent. Even actual spies were few and far between and hardly needed actual tactical surveillance techniques. Despite their insistence, she stuck with it. Perhaps it was the influence of her father's story she heard as a young girl. When he was in the Underground, surveillance was all they had to rely on to stay alive and fight back.

A flashing in the corner of her eye caught her attention and pulled her out of her thoughts. An alert on the computer screen blinked rapidly. Ignoring the frustration directed at her from the most recent driver trying to make it through her checkpoint, she turned to look more closely. The tag on Rahim's car had created an alert. The car had received a traffic violation for being parked in a No Parking zone on Maple Street. She didn't know the area well enough to be able to picture if it was a residential or commercial street. Dearborn was about a ninety-minute drive away, just south of Detroit. Certainty not a hunting area up north.

She turned her attention back on her immediate responsibilities while the back of her mind remained fixated on the new knowledge. It gave her a more precise location, but not much else. Her next step had to be a closer, more consistent means of surveillance. The office at the bridge didn't have anything like that. They were not legally allowed to put GPS trackers on cars without warrants, since it was considered a breach of civil liberties. Anything she did independently would be shady at best and downright illegal at its worst. She would have to be strategic about how she moved forward.

Anna stepped out of her car a few blocks from where Rahim had received his traffic citation. As soon as her shift was over, she had made her way to the uniform lockers and checked out a blue field uniform and patrol car. The process for signing out the things she needed was simple. She told them that she was going to check up on a traffic violation involving a person of interest she had flagged, which was mostly true, if not the whole truth. She buttoned up the uniform and hopped into the cruiser without even heading home.

About halfway to Dearborn, she felt her cell phone vibrate. She knew without looking at it that her father was wondering why she wasn't home yet. She clicked it off for the time being to buy her time to come up with an excuse.

When she pulled into Dearborn, she felt her heart rate increase, and the sweat on her palms made her fingers slip along the steering wheel. It was one thing to listen to her daddy's stories of espionage and study surveillance in school, but, as she realized now, it was another thing to engage in it against the mandate of her superiors.

The disguise she wore was far from perfect. The border patrol car had green stripping on the side with lettering that indicated where it came from, but it was the same make and model as police cars, and with the lights on top, most people didn't think twice about the inherent authority it implied. Her uniform was blue rather than the standard green. As long as no one looked too closely at the badges, they wouldn't be able to distinguish her from a real traffic cop. She just needed to get close enough to the car—if she was able to find it.

She parked the car and got out to walk a few blocks from where Rahim's car had received the citation. The car was great for getting through traffic, but it would only be a big warning to Rahim if he saw it. The neighborhood looked quaint and clean, with small, single-family homes lined up in neat little rows, standing on their own little patches of grass. As she walked, she passed a huge football field that must have belonged to Fordson High School, where kids were running drills accompanied by the coaches' screams to move faster and work harder. She smiled at the quintessential picture of Middle America. The sun reached its early evening rays across the sky, highlighting the white picket fences with kids playing in the yards. She enjoyed her brisk stroll, allowing her mind a brief break from the task ahead.

She kept an eye on the passing street signs and house numbers, and as she got closer, she pulled out a notepad. She made a show of looking at each meter to see if it had expired while simultaneously peeking at the makes, models, and license plates to see if any of them matched her guy. She walked the length of the block where the citation occurred without any luck. She paused briefly in her disappointment, leaning against a gray Camry with her arms folded. If she didn't have any luck

here, she wasn't sure what her next move would be. Signing out the car
and uniform again to play this little charade seemed unlikely to fly. As
it was, she might face a talking to or worse when she got back.

She scanned the neighborhood again, wondering if this was where
he had settled or if it was simply a stop along the way to somewhere else.
It seemed like a strange place to stop for a rest. There weren't any stores
or gas stations within sight. Her gaze landed on a car across the street.
It was the right color, and from where she stood, it looked like the right
make. She looked around with fresh suspicious eyes this time, scanning
for anyone who might be out of place. She crossed the street and played
traffic cop again, starting a few cars down from the one she really wanted
to look at. The street was mostly empty, but she would need some time
to do what she needed to do.

She stepped up beside the car. The license plate matched. This was
it. Her heart pounded again as her nerves increased, threatening to end
the mission. She took a deep breath to steady herself. She hadn't come
this far to give up. She had brought with her a professional grade satellite
GPS tracker with a magnetic mount. She could have simply slid it under
the car and been done with it, but she couldn't risk it coming off. She
had to get it in the car and under the seat. She studied the car. It was an
older model, but new enough to have an alarm system. She would have
to disable the alarm as soon as she popped the lock.

Reaching into her utility belt, she pulled out a wedge and a probe.
Sliding the wedge into the top of the window, she wiggled it down just
enough to slide the probe in while keeping her eyes constantly shifted on
her surroundings. Her hands felt slick along the thin metal of the probe,
and she felt a light drop of sweat trickle down her forehead. She moved
the probe around until it hooked on the lock. She pulled it up as the
horn started blaring, breaking through the silence. Without hesitating,

she pulled open the door, slid her hand under the steering wheel and pulled the plastic casing off to expose the wires. With a swift tug, she disconnected the alarm.

Sighing with relief, she took a quick look around to see how much attention she had attracted. A few scattered pedestrians walked the sidewalks without so much as looking in her direction. Toward the end of the street, a man with dark skin, wearing a camouflage-colored baseball cap, walked casually in her direction. She couldn't be sure it was him, but a new panic overwhelmed her. Her fingers fumbled with her side belt for the GPS tracking device. As she ripped it free of its too-small pocket, she peeked up at the man's progress. He was approaching quicker than she thought he would at what looked like a slow pace from further away. Now that he was closer, it looked more like a brisk speed walk. She ducked back into the car and reached under the front driver's seat. The magnet engaged with the metal underneath the seat, securing it in place.

Her fingers searched the sides of the box, not much larger than a silver dollar, for the small switch that would initiate the tracking device. She could have kicked herself for not turning it on before she put it in place. Rooky mistake. The hair on the back of her neck stood up, and her skin prickled with anticipation as she imagined the man she had seen walking up and finder her tampering with his car. She finally found the switch and pushed it to the on position. She stuffed the wires she had pulled out back into the steering wheel casing and snapped the cover on. With a single fluid motion, she stood, closed the door and moved seamlessly away from the car to look back at the notepad she had been carrying before. She stepped to the next car down the line, checking the meter as the man approached his car.

From the corner of her eye, she instantly recognized him. The man climbed into his car without even sparing her a glance and drove away.

That had been dangerously close, but elation flooded her at the success, and she couldn't help but smile. She began the walk back to her car, pulling out her phone and initializing the app for the tracker. After a moment of waiting, a map appeared on her screen with a green icon representing Rahim's car. She skipped with delight as a yip of excitement escaped her lips. She had done it. It must have been in her DNA. A smile spread on her lips as she wondered if her dad would approve of her skills now that she was all grown up.

All of her waking hours outside of work became consumed with tracking the suspect's movements. She created a log of where he went, how often and how long he stayed there. With each stop, she tried to pinpoint the location of the car on a map that she had hung up in her room, above her wooden desk that had been there since she was a little girl. Her small bedroom in the corner of her parent's farmhouse wasn't the best place for her recon headquarters, but she would make it work. She studied the map around the areas that his car would park for long stretches, but without having a GPS connected directly to his person, there was no way to know exactly where he went each time the car stopped.

She rested her elbows on the desk and cradled her head in her hands. Her excitement at succeeding in attaching the GPS had quickly turned to frustration when she realized it wasn't enough. She had quickly assessed that he was staying somewhere close to Maple Street, since his car would park overnight on the same stretch of road each night. The other places he went were out of Anna's reach from her distant surveillance.

She lifted her head to look at the map with a determined expression. She wasn't about to give up now without a fight. She stood up, grabbed her jacket and headed for the door.

"Hey? Where are you going?" Ivan asked, as she walked past the living room where he sat in front of the TV, watching the latest college football game.

"Oh, just out."

"Just out?" He turned his full attention on her. "You have been out a lot lately, and you didn't come hunting last weekend. What is going on with you?"

"Nothing, I am just trying to make a good impression at work by taking on some extra stuff." She hated lying to her brother. She had never lied to anyone in her family before, but she knew that if they so much as suspected that she had gone rogue to find a potentially dangerous suspect, they would lock her in her room for the rest of her life. She loved her whole family dearly, but all of them, especially her father, felt it was their job to keep her safe at all times. They wouldn't understand why she was doing this alone or trust that she could handle it without their supervision.

Ivan squinted, trying to decide if he believed her or not. Her past honesty worked in her favor. "All right, but make sure you are free for this weekend's hunting trip," he said.

"I won't miss it," she said with a smile as she stepped out the front door.

Through the closed door, she heard her father questioning Ivan. She paused to listen.

"She is going out again?" her father asked.

"I guess so," Ivan said.

"Where is she going?"

"I don't know."

"Why not? That is your job as the big brother," her father chided before she heard his loud footsteps walking back toward the kitchen. He was probably heading out, back to his secret room in the barn. He went there whenever he was worried.

Anna quickly finished her walk to her car. The gravel crunched under her tires as she pulled out onto I-94 west.

She sped through Michigan, making record time, and was flooded with relief when she saw Rahim's car still parked on Maple Street where it had been when she left home. She pulled into an empty spot as the sun was starting to set and hunkered down in her seat, watching Rahim's car while keeping an eye on the surroundings.

About an hour into her stakeout, she stifled a yawn as her eyelids started getting heavy. The thrill of adventure had worn off, and she struggled to keep her focus sharp. She pictured her father as a young man back in Russia. Would he have done things like this? Possibly holding one of those huge clunky audio dishes seen in the old movies, with giant over-the-ear headphones as he tried to listen in on secret meetings. The thought made her smile. Maybe she should invest in an audio device. Why hadn't she thought of that before?

She couldn't spend too long on the thought because she noticed a man, who from afar may have been Rahim, walk down the small front porch of one of the houses. Anna squinted to see the mailbox number before refocusing on who she thought might be Rahim. When he reached his car, she knew it was him. She turned on her own ignition and waited for him to pull out before easing out of her own spot. Her car remained a few car lengths back so he wouldn't become alarmed. They drove through the residential area of the city to a location that Anna hadn't seen on the GPS tracker before. Her stomach tied in knots as she contemplated all the ways this scenario could potentially play out. If it ended in a shootout, she had a pretty good chance of survival, as long as she could actually pull the trigger when facing a person instead of a deer. She took a deep breath to steady herself. *Stay calm,* she told herself.

Rahim pulled up to a four-way stop, and she had no choice but to pull up directly behind him while they both waited for their turn to go. Lines of cars waited on each side. Without using a turn signal, he made a right. She grumbled under her breath about how rude and even dangerous his lack of blinker was as she pulled up to the stop sign.

She waited to make the turn, making sure her own turn signal indicated her direction. She drummed her fingers on the wheel impatiently, worried she would lose him at the busy intersection. If she didn't have eyes on him, she would miss his final destination and be no better off than when she was sitting at her desk at home. Across the way, a black SUV with an older gentleman with silver hair, wearing a stern expression, waved her in front of him. She smiled and waved her thanks as she coasted down the street. The black car followed her down the street, which was crowded with cars. She spotted Rahim's car parked in a small lot beside what looked like a community center. Her eyes scanned the small groups of people filtering into the building before they landed on Rahim. He smiled and shook hands with another man about his age.

As she turned her eyes back to the road, Rahim looked up from the conversation he was having to see a Jeep Grand Cherokee drive by with a young blonde girl in the driver's seat. He looked back to his friend before recognition dawned in his mind.

CHAPTER SEVEN

V-MAN WAVED THE YOUNG GIRL THROUGH THE
stop sign before taking the turn behind her and pulling into the parking
lot attached to the event hall. The party was being held at the newly
constructed Arabic community center on a plot of land that had once
held a crumbling tenement building. The construction had stirred up
a lot of controversy at the time, but V-man didn't mind. The architec-
ture was unobtrusive, they kept the area clean, and they provided some
community services to the town. V-man hadn't had a reason to be inside
it until today.

Beside him, his middle son, Luca, looking dapper in the newly
bought suit and combed back hair, climbed out of the car. V-man had a
wife and three boys, but his boys had become mostly grown men somewhere along the way. V-man caught up with Luca around the back
of the SUV.

"You know, you should really wear a suit more often," V-man said,
putting his arm around his shoulder.

"What would I wear a suit to?" Luca said. He took after his father.
He might have only been five feet, seven inches, but what he lacked
in stature he made up for in Italian attitude. Looking at him was like
looking into the past, for V-man. It was hard to believe that there was

a time that he worried Luca wouldn't make it to see his third birthday, but here he was, practically a grown man.

"You would wear it to work or out on dates," V-man said.

Luca shook his head and laughed. "You are showing your age, Dad." The pair walked into the community center. Since Luca had moved out, V-man felt like he didn't spend enough time with his son. He had lived at home through college, but as soon as he got his first job, he had found a small apartment with a few high school friends, one of whom was the reason they were at the party that night. He had a good work ethic and was putting away some money in the bank. V-man was glad for the opportunity to spend an evening with him.

The open foyer of the community center was brightly lit and decorated in flashy colors that threatened to overwhelm visitors not used to the decorating aesthetic. People milled about the lobby before slowly funneling into the main event room. Standing close to the doorway, the host and hostess stood, greeting all the guests who came in. Amesh and Napor were of Middle Eastern decent, Chaldean Iraqi Christians. One of Luca's roommates, Jasim, was having some sort of traditional religious coming-of-age ceremony. They reminded V-man of the early Italians who had settled in the Detroit area: hard working, dedicated to family, strict Catholics, and loyal friends. V-man also knew there were some radicals in the area, but they kept an extremely low profile.

V-man and Amesh went way back. One night when Luca was only two years old, he got sick. V-man and his wife assumed it was just a cold until Luca started turning blue and his breaths came in short little gasps. When they rushed him to the emergency room, the doctors huddled around them, wanting to run tests to try to figure out the strange symptoms. A younger Amesh pushed through the crowd in his blue scrubs, took one look at Luca and said, "Epiglottitis." That one word was so full of confidence that everyone stopped and listened. Epiglottitis was a deadly rare virus that attacked the throat and was treatable only if caught early enough. Amesh worked quickly without doubt to run a tube down Luca's small closed-off throat. The effects were instantaneous. Luca breathed easier, and his color came back. From that point on, V-man and Amesh became close friends. Saving his son's life wasn't something he could ever repay adequately. Through their friendship, their sons bonded with the normal interests that young boys and teenagers have.

"Hey, man, nice place you got here," V-man said, reaching out his hand in greeting. Amesh shook V-man's with a smile.

"Thank you, my friend," he said. "We are quite pleased with how it turned out. We are excited to be the first ones to use it for a celebration."

"So where is the man of the hour?" V-man asked, looking around and realizing he had lost his own son, too.

"Oh, they must have found the recreational room. It is filled with some entertaining things."

V-man was always amused by how formally Amesh spoke.

"Sounds nice," V-man said, nodding in appreciation. Besides Amesh, a man who stood a few inches taller than Amesh watched them speaking.

When Amesh noticed him, he waved him over with a friendly gesture. "Here, let me introduce you to my house guest. V-man, this is Rahim. Rahim, this is my good friend, V-man."

Rahim bowed his head slightly with his hands folded in front of him, rather than offering his hand to shake. "It is nice to meet you. I have never heard a name like V-man before."

"Not many people have. It's a nickname I got in Vietnam," V-man said.

"It is very . . . American," Rahim said, with what looked to V-man like a forced smile. His accent was thick, and he said the word *American* as if it was a bad thing. V-man lifted an eyebrow as he considered the man standing in front of him. A scraggly beard formed around his jaw line, and his hair was buzzed close to his head. "You fought in Vietnam?"

"Yes, I did," V-man said. "With pride and resolve. It is an honor to serve my country."

Rahim shook his head. "It is just a shame that the US keeps entering into wars where it doesn't belong and can't seem to finish."

V-man's expression darkened. He had a natural tendency to automatically dislike anyone who came to his country and didn't show it the proper respect, but to start openly criticizing the policy decisions was more than V-man could take. He had watched too many young men lose their lives in Vietnam to have some stranger come in and assume he knew better.

"We did our duty to our country. The country that is kind enough to take you in and provide you comfort as you vacation here. You should not bring that attitude here." V-man took a deep breath. He didn't want to ruin Amesh's party by throwing down with his house guest, but in any other situation, he might have. He saw the worried expression on Amesh's face as his gaze darted quickly between the two men. "What brings you to the States anyway, Rahim?" V-man asked, trying to defuse the situation.

"I wanted to spend some time seeing the world before I got married myself. I think it is important to learn other cultures," Rahim said.

"Insulting them doesn't seem like the best way to learn anything about them. You may want to have a more open mind for the rest of your trip," V-man said. He tilted his head toward Amesh and made his departure.

While he walked the room, he never let Rahim out of his sight. His skin tingled as a thought itched at the back of his mind. Something about Rahim made V-man's stomach turn. He had learned over the years to trust the gut-twisting feeling. It had yet to steer him in the wrong direction. He sipped the drink that he had found as his eyes followed Rahim. On the outside, there was nothing unusual about the man. He mingled with a friendly smile as he chatted or introduced himself. As he made his way around the room, a pattern began to develop. Rahim only seemed interested in talking to the other Middle Easterners at the party. At first V-man thought he was jumping to conclusions that Rahim wasn't avoiding the other guests on purpose, but rather just so happened to only come in contact with the ones who resembled himself. V-man shifted his position near the refreshment table, trying to both look occupied, gathering hors d'oeurves onto a plate, while also getting himself a better view of Rahim's movements. As he studied him with closer scrutiny, he realized that Amesh's guest subtly maneuvered his body through the crowd in order to position himself to remain only in the line of sight of those guests that most likely shared his belief system or some form of it anyway.

V-man could have given him the benefit of the doubt, that he was simply shy and wanted to avoid an uncomfortable conversation with people he didn't know, but he thought that would be far too generous. Rahim came to a stop at a table set up with a variety of drinks, where his son and his friend, Jasim, stood chatting. V-man hadn't noticed them rejoin the party. They both looked happy while they spoke, laughing about something only they found funny, reminding V-man of when they were just kids. It seemed like a lifetime ago. The pleasant nostalgia that occupied him for a moment faded into a new anxiety as Rahim stepped in between them. He spoke a few words and nodded his head off toward a hallway on the far side of the room. Luca nodded hesitantly and stepped away in the direction Rahim had nodded.

V-man was torn between the desire to find out where his son had been sent and watching Rahim and Jasim's interaction. There must have been a reason that Luca was sent away, but was the reason primarily to get Jasim alone or to send Luca somewhere specific? As he debated, he watched Jasim's expression change. What had started as a friendly smile turned into something more. His eyes widened, and he nodded his head quickly up and down with emphatic agreement for whatever Rahim was saying. Rahim placed a hand on Jasim's shoulder as he spoke, and Jasim's adoration seemed to double. V-man felt his stomach turn again as he watched the interaction. It just added volume to his already blaring alarm bells. A young man like Jasim should not be so easily taken in by a man like Rahim.

Out of the corner of his eye, he caught movement and realized it was his son. He quickly left his post beside the food table to catch him before he rejoined his friend. He stepped into his son's path about halfway through the open room, catching him off guard.

"Oh, hey Dad," Luca said.

"Where did you go?" V-man asked.

"Oh, we were checking out the rest of the facility. It is pretty cool. They actually have an indoor pool here. Jasim said he would take me back sometime for some laps," his son said.

"Sounds nice, but where were you just now?" V-man said.

"Getting more ice for the drink buckets." Luca said it like it was obvious as he held up two bags of ice in either hand. V-man had been so focused on Rahim that he hadn't really taken note of what his son had.

"Why?" V-man asked. "I thought you were a guest here?"

"Relax, Dad," Luca said, recognizing the initial signs of his dad's habit of over-analyzing almost every situation. "Jasim's friend, or whatever he is, asked if I could grab it. I said yes."

"What do you know about Rahim?" V-man asked, glancing in their direction again. They hadn't moved from their previous position. Their heads were bent closer together in a conspiratorial whisper.

"Nothing, really. He is staying with Jasim and his family. Jasim hasn't been home much since Rahim has been here, I guess he feels obligated to spend time at home visiting and stuff."

"How does he know the family?"

"Dad, I really don't know much about any of it. These bags are getting kind of heavy," he said, lifting the bags for emphasis. "I will talk to you later."

V-man sighed in frustration but let him go without another word. When Luca rejoined Rahim and Jasim, their demeanor changed instantly. They stepped back from each other, and the hero worship left Jasim's face as his expression turned back into a simple smile, happy to see his friend. Together they refilled the buckets of ice before separating from Rahim and disappearing into the depths of the facility again. V-man kept eyes on Rahim until he stepped down a side hallway and didn't come back again for the rest of the night. He remained absent even during the formal part of the evening's ceremony, although no one else appeared to miss his absence.

The party wound down. V-man and Luca said their goodbyes and exited for the parking lot. The street lamps had turned on while they were inside. Beyond their small pools of light, the night created a penetrating darkness. The sound of their footfalls echoed through the lot, one of the only sounds aside from the random car engine the roared down the street.

"That was fun, thanks for coming, Dad," Luca said.

"It was nice," V-man replied, although his eyes remained sharp on their surroundings.

"Maybe we can . . ." Luca's voice trailed off as V-man raised his hand to get his attention. Luca looked around curiously.

V-man had heard some hushed voices and stopped to listen. In a dark corner beside the building, he saw two figures talking. He hurried Luca to the SUV where he ducked out of sight, while still keeping eyes on the pair of men. As his eyes adjusted to the darkness, he recognized Jasim and Rahim. He cursed under his breath in frustration that he couldn't make out what they were saying beyond vague mumbles. What looked like a book bag passed between their hands, and then the exchange ended as quickly as it had started. Jasim made his way back into the building with the backpack slung over his shoulder while Rahim hurried back to his car and sped away. This left V-man even more confident than before that he had to keep an eye on the developing situation.

CHAPTER EIGHT

ANNA FOUND HERSELF SITTING OUTSIDE WHAT
had once been an elementary school in a sketchier part of Detroit.
Graffiti covered most of the brick surfaces, and the windows looked
to have little glass left in them, while the jungle gym rusted to dust on
an overgrown patch of grass. Overhead, the sun burnt in oranges and
purples as it climbed the horizon, leaving dark shadows around her that
wouldn't fade until the sun reached a higher point. The only familiar
sight was Rahim's car, half-hidden behind the far side of the school. This
was one of her first days off, and she wanted to use the opportunity to
see what her suspect did during the day, rather than in the evening hours.

For the first time during her reconnaissance, she started having
second thoughts. Why had Rahim driven to a long-abandoned school?
For all her planning, she didn't have a contingency for what would
happen if she came face-to-face with a large terrorist cell. Her preparations only accounted for the eventuality of finding evidence that he
was a suspect, so she could present it to her higher-ups, and they could
call in the cavalry.

Her car rolled to a stop on the opposite side of the building from
Rahim's. The sound of the car door as it opened echoed across the barren
landscape, too loud to her ears. Closing it gently, she crouch-walked to

the trunk and popped it open. Unlike her brothers, she didn't carry an arsenal with her everywhere she went, but she had promised she would join the hunting trip today, so before her excursion, she had packed up all her gear, including her 30–30 Henry Repeating hunting rifle. For close combat, it would be too bulky and cumbersome. Instead, she pulled out her Sig Sauer P 320 9mm Government issue M-9 service pistol. She was an excellent shot regardless of which weapon she used. With a quick prayer that she wouldn't have to use it, she crept around the building, taking her time to peek into every window and keep an eye behind her. She had learned a long time ago how to walk in silence and keep herself hidden despite the sparse covering. Luckily, the pavement that surrounded the school was cracked and broken, filled in with weeds and grass trying to take back the landscape. It cushioned her steps and aided in her stealth.

She made her way along the long side of the building without incident or signs of any life. When she reached the corner, Rahim's car was abandoned, but no other cars had joined it, which was a relief. With her back pressed against the rough brick wall, she ventured a peek further around the corner. There was nothing to see except more of the same deteriorating school.

She hesitated. She had two choices. The first was to continue pursuing Rahim into the sketchy building, risking her own wellbeing to finally get proof of his underhanded dealings. Or she could cut her losses, go home, and guarantee her own safety. The rational, well-trained side of her nagged her to leave. The competitive side of her urged her to keep going, unwilling to forfeit the potential discovery that laid ahead. After a long moment of indecision, she rounded the corner. The chain that had previously held the double doors closed hung loose from one of the door's handles, with the rusted, broken lock lying on the ground underneath. Her fingers pocketed the lock. She wanted to look more closely at what was used to break it when she had more time.

Staying beneath the window, she inched inside the building. The halls were deserted, littered with long-discarded papers and textbooks. It felt like the scene out of a post-apocalyptic movie with the early rays of the sun giving everything a dull grey color. She quickly moved to the side and pressed herself up against the tiles that lined the wall. Standing in the empty halls, she was completely vulnerable with nothing to hide behind. Her best bet was to make her way to the first classroom. She would case the building quickly, then exit out the other side closest to her car. Some classroom doors stood half open, others were closed, while a few looked like they had broken off the hinges either partially or completely.

The first doorway stood closed only a few feet away. Her feet scraped through the dust that had accumulated on the floor through years of neglect as she approached. Her fingers reached for the handle before she paused. Something wasn't right. In front of her feet, the dust had been streaked. Her head tilted to the side, so she could look for any footprints besides her own, but she didn't see any. The uneven dust in front of her was an indication that the door had recently stood open. Someone must be in the room. But why? She had to get a better view. She slowly began shuffling backward, not wanting to take her eyes off the door, intent on back tracking and looking through the outside window again. Before she made it a full step, the door flung open abruptly, slamming into her face. She cursed her hesitation under her breath as her back hit the linoleum floor, knocking the air out of her lungs and the gun out of her hand. Through the window, Rahim smiled wickedly at her.

"You are out of your league, girl," he said in a low, hissing voice.

She stayed on the ground and put her hands in front of her face. Blood from her nose dripped onto her palm. Then she began to cry. "Oh, please, please don't hurt me," she sobbed in her best impression of a damsel in distress. She heard his laughter coming closer. "You are right. I shouldn't have come. I just thought I could impress everyone at work, so they wouldn't think I was just a stupid girl."

"Too bad you are just a stupid girl," he said. Through the gaps in her fingers, she saw him come around the door and start reaching for her. In a split second, she swung her elbow around, smashing it into her assailant's face with a sickening crack. Blood sprayed across her face. Pressing her hands on the floor behind her, she did a back flip to land softly on her feet. The pistol had come to a stop a few steps behind Rahim. She eyed the pistol debating the best way to make a lunge for it.

"While your inherent bias may have helped me this time, I suggest you don't go around underestimating American women anymore," she spat at him. "I am taking you in." Rahim had been knocked to the floor by her hit, and now he was scuttling backward on hands and feet. He kicked with one leg, forcing Anna to swerve a block. Rahim didn't seem to have as much hand-to-hand training as she did, so it wasn't hard to maneuver, but it gave him just enough time to reach back and grab her firearm off the floor and aim it in her direction. The sound of the safety clicking off echoed down the hall.

Anna's heart lurched in her chest at the inevitability that he would use the gun without hesitation. Instinctively, she fell into an offensive stance as she threw her leg forward in a side kick. Her foot landed on Rahim's wrist throwing his arm off the side. Without thinking, she pushed the hand holding the gun downward while twisting the gun backward. It was a move that she had learning in hand-to-hand but never thought she would actually need. When she brought the pistol up, she was looking down the barrel of Rahim's handgun that he had pulled from behind him with his free hand.

She threw herself into the open classroom beside her and threw the door closed, as a shot rang out in the hallway. She aimed the gun at one of outer windows and fired three quick rounds. The glass shattered and fell from its frame. That would buy her a few precious seconds. Clicking on the safety and shoving the gun into the back of her jeans, she tucked and rolled through the new opening, onto the hard-concrete outside. Her shoulder would probably be sore for weeks, along with her nose. She crouched onto one knee and sighted into the classroom for a moment. There was no sign of movement.

She took the opportunity to rise to her feet and sprint for her car. The thought of leaving him behind to continue whatever scheming he intended to do made her sick to her stomach, but he had clearly lured her here with the intent to kill her, and without the proper weapon, she wasn't sure she would make it out alive. If she died now, then he would definitely be free to carry out whatever plot he intended.

Her failure stuck in her head during the long drive home. She was more determined than ever to figure out what Rahim was hiding.

"Is she coming?" Buddy asked as he unpacked his hunting rifle and began inspecting the barrels.

"She said she was," Ivan said, although the raise of his eyebrows indicated that he wasn't one hundred percent sure he believed that.

"Where has she been lately?"

"I don't know. Ever since she started her job, she has been gone all the time."

"I thought you guys always knew where your sister was," Jimmy said.

"We used to," Pavlo said. He pulled his hunting jacket on and fixed hit baseball cap.

The two trucks were parked in a deserted parking lot that had been overrun by moss, grass, and weeds a long time ago. When the boys were in elementary school, they had gone exploring on their bikes one day and came across the parking lot at the end of a well-hidden dirt road. At first they thought they were on private property and sped off quickly before someone caught them, but their curiosity led them back again and again before they found out it had once been the main parking lot for the local state park before it had become too small and they moved the parking lot and visitors center to a more frequently traveled road.

The boys had quickly adopted the hidden spot as their official hideout, building forts out of sticks and camping out overnight. When they got older, it transformed into the perfect hunting place. They never had to worry about other hunters or crowds.

The guys had unloaded the trucks quickly and looked around, uncertain if they should start walking to their tree house or if they should stick around and wait for Anna.

"Let's just go," Pavlo said. He was the younger of the two brothers and was always more impulsive than Ivan.

"I think we should wait," Ivan said.

"She is a big girl. She will find her way. Besides, she might not even come. We could be waiting all day for her."

Ivan sighed, looking uncomfortably torn. He opened his mouth to speak but was interrupted by a crackling noise. He looked over to Buddy with the start of a smile.

Buddy looked down at the long-range walkie-talkie on his belt that was crackling with static. He brought it to his mouth and pushed the button before speaking. "Hello?"

"Hey there, Bud, just checking in." His dad's voice came through the line with a lot of static, indicating that he was probably on a pretty far drive.

Buddy's cheeks flushed a light red as they always did when he was caught talking to his daddy while with his friends. "Everything is good, Dad. Where are you at today?"

"I am on the Dearborn–Ann Arbor–Monroe route for the next few days. It is a slog, but not as bad as some of the others."

Buddy's dad drove a big rig for the local dairy farms that supplied fresh milk, cheese, and yogurt throughout most of Michigan and beyond. Their area of Michigan was well known for the dairy farms. He made it a habit of staying in near constant contact with Buddy during his route. The guys ribbed him endlessly for being a daddy's boy, even though they were all close to their own families as well.

When Buddy got off the phone, Jimmy, Pavlo, and Ivan all shared a look before bursting out in laughter. Buddy shook his head and threw a playful punch at Pavlo, who happened to be standing closest to him.

"Uh oh, is Daddy going to be home to tuck you in tonight, Buddy?" Jimmy asked in a mock baby voice.

"Who is gonna tell you a bedtime story?" Pavlo chimed in.

"You guys are assholes. There is nothing wrong with me checking in with my dad," Buddy said.

The conversation quickly died as they heard gravel crunching, indicating an approaching car.

"Finally," Ivan said, but when the car came into sight, they realized it wasn't Anna's. Instead the old tan-and-cream-colored Ford pickup that their father drove rumbled down the drive. The truck was about as old as Anna herself. Their father had bought it new and cherished it ever since as a sign of his frugal beginnings.

"Ha!" Buddy said with vindication. "Now who needs their daddy?"

Everyone ignored him as Olek climbed out of the truck. For an older man, he was still spry and fit. He pulled his rifle off the rack, followed by a duffle bag of equipment.

"Hey, Pops," Pavlo said, reaching into the truck to help his father unload a cooler. "Didn't think you would make it out today."

"I heard Anna might make a rare appearance, and I didn't want to miss it," he said with his usual jovial smile.

The other guys shared a regretful look.

"Let me guess; she isn't here yet?" Olek asked, shaking his head. "We might as well get started setting up camp."

With the efficiency of a task done countless times before, they trudged through the woods with their hunting gear and set up in the nest they had built. Each one spent time with their rifle and gear in silence, moving through individualized rituals designed to make the hunting productive.

"She isn't simply spending time with friends," Olek said, breaking the silence as if he knew that for certain.

"What?" Ivan asked, as worry crept into his voice.

"How do you know?" Pavlo asked at the same time.

"Back in the Ukraine," he began. Pavlo and Ivan sighed and settled back against the uneven wood of the hideout, prepared for a lengthy story. "I was a young man of only sixteen or seventeen, when I noticed my neighbor's strange behavior. At that age, I already had a bit of a rebellious streak, going out later than I should have and the like. When I saw my neighbor sneaking off under cover of darkness, I naively followed. With no experience in espionage and no sense of the danger, I haphazardly threw myself into the middle of something much bigger than myself. It eventually, of course, led to my recruitment in the Underground, but during that period, I made up thinly veiled lies to tell my family. They had their own troubles, so they didn't spend much energy worrying about where I was at night, but in truth, I was never around.

"Now the same thing happened when I met your mother. I would sneak off with some excuse of productive work but instead visited her. Back in those days, relationships between Ukrainian men and Russian women were frowned upon, especially if the Ukrainian man happened to be a member of the Underground, hell bent on overthrowing the Iron Curtain. So your sister has either gotten herself into some deep shit, or she has met a boy that she doesn't think we would approve of."

Ivan and Pavlo sat dumbfounded, with their mouths hanging open at their father's suggestion.

"No," Ivan said. "I can't believe that. Who could she have found that we wouldn't approve of?"

"Just about anyone," Buddy said with a laugh beside him. "You guys are pretty strict with her."

"Being protective does not mean we are strict," Pavlo said defensively.

They turned their attention back to the forest, contemplating the implications of Anna's sudden scarcity. A rustling through the leaves drew their attention, and five rifles all lifted at once, aiming toward the noise.

"Just me," Anna's voice called, followed by her bright orange vest with her hands raised innocently in the air. She had stopped at home before coming out, to clean up and put makeup on her nose. Luckily, the bruising hadn't started yet, so it was just a little red that she hoped wouldn't be noticeable.

"You should know better than sneaking up on us, Anna," Ivan chided.

"Sorry I'm late," she said, climbing up into the nest. "I had a thing at work I had to finish up."

She was met with silence and skeptical looks.

"Why all the tension?" she asked, settling herself in. The nest hadn't really been made for six people, but they weren't ready to split up just yet.

"A thing?" Pavlo asked.

She glanced sideways at his accusatory tone, then met the gazes of the rest of the guys. Her father looked mildly amused, while Ivan looked hurt and offended. Buddy and Jimmy held worry in their expressions.

"Yes. A thing," Anna said defiantly.

"We know the truth!" Ivan said.

"What?" Anna asked, as her tone rose sharply in alarm.

"We know that you met a boy," Ivan said.

Anna kept a straight face as long as she possibly could before she burst into laughter. "Why would I lie about that?"

Ivan looked sheepish. "Then what is it? Why are you always out and not telling us? Are you doing something illegal?"

"I wouldn't say illegal . . ."

CHAPTER NINE

"NOW THERE'S ANOTHER THING I WANT YOU TO remember. I don't want to get any messages saying that 'we are holding our position.' We're not holding anything. Let the Hun do that. We are advancing constantly, and we're not interested in holding onto anything except the enemy. We're going to hold onto him by the nose, and we're going to kick him in the ass. We're going to kick the hell out of him all the time, and we're going to go through him like crap through a goose!"

The sound of Patton's voice blasted from the small iPad speakers, drowning out any other noise in the small corner of the bar occupied by V-man. V-man's voice, reciting the same lines, reached the other corners of the bar that the iPad couldn't get to.

V-man drank his coffee and ate his eggs over easy with white toast. By now, the rest of the regulars at the bar could probably recite the same lines. V-man liked the daily reminder of his underlying purpose in life. To fight for his country in whatever form that took. Back in Vietnam, it meant strapping himself into the chopper and cutting down the Viet-Cong. Afterward, it meant raising his children to be God-fearing, patriotic Americans. Now he turned that duty onto the vets coming home from the Middle East and keeping an eye on his neighborhood.

His buddies at the bar had their own way of being patriotic, although not everyone saw it the same way V-man did. The corner bar, to a lot of the customers, was just a place to sit and eat some good food with some good beer and good friends. To V-man, it was a vestige of quintessential American life, where two guys who came from nothing could create something important to the community. It was a safe place to go with the two Monsters of the Midway at their back.

When AC and Big Mike first got together, a few foolish tough guys in the community saw it as a challenge, thinking those two old guys were past their prime. One night, five muscled-up guys sauntered into the bar while Babinski sat, eating his pigs in a blanket. Two of the guys sat down at a table while the other three walked up to the bar. The room was thick with tension as everyone in the place recognized the intent of the meatheads making a presence of themselves.

Brenda stepped up hesitantly to the table. "What can I get you?"

"Well, sweetheart, I doubt there is anything in this dump that could satisfy me. Judging from the looks o' you, I think I might be right," the guy said, nudging his buddy with an elbow as they shared a laugh.

Brenda didn't bat an eye at the insult. She had seen enough in her days not to get flustered by some little punk-ass kids. Behind her, Babinski wiped his mouth with a napkin before slowly rising out of his chair, and AC stepped out from the back room. It only took a second for him to assess the situation.

The whole fight didn't last more than three minutes. Babinski stepped up alongside the one who had spoken to Brenda and threw an amazingly fast left hook that turned the guy's lights out before he hit the ground. The guy sitting at the table beside him reacted quickly, grabbing a beer bottle and smashing it over Mike's head. Mike paused only a moment before picking the guy up and throwing him across the tables to land on the opposite side of the room.

AC grabbed one guy by the neck, practically fitting the entire width of it in one hand and threw him to the ground. He straightened quickly to throw a punch at another approaching guy. The fist landed with a sickening crack on his jaw. He clutched his face, groaning. Behind them, V-man, who had been watching the whole thing, calmly walked up slowly to one of the unoccupied thugs, and with swift efficiency flipped him to the ground in a choke hold. He didn't have the brawn that his friends had, but what he lacked in muscle he made up for in swift, cunning ruthlessness.

AC and Big Mike ushered the offensive patrons out of the bar, throwing them to the pavement outside. The other customers in the bar had watched with wide eyes. Undoubtedly, when they left, they spread the word about the day's altercation, exaggerating it to an epic battle in which the bar's owners came across as superhuman heroes. When AC and Big Mike walked back in the bar, V-man was sitting calmly in his spot again.

"You know, I had to get myself a beer. You guys should do something about the service in here," he said with a smile.

Big Mike laughed heartily. "How about I buy everyone a round?" he said, loudly enough for the entire bar to hear.

The patrons in the bar shouted with excitement. They probably would have paid good money to see the show they had just witnessed but getting a free round on top of it solidified it as a night to remember.

AC shook his head, eyeing the V-man. It didn't come as a surprise that he somehow managed to always be in the middle of all the action. No matter where the excitement was or who was involved, anyone who looked closely enough would always see V-man in the mix somewhere.

He wondered quietly if perhaps V-man had invited the ruffians to the bar just to stir things up. It wasn't outside of the realm of possibilities where V-man was concerned.

After the incident with the fight, no one challenged Big Mike or AC again, except maybe the law, in an effort to carry out old grudges.

V-man finished reciting his lines from Patton. He felt it was his duty to educate his friends on the words of wisdom and strength from an American great. Behind him, someone turned the TV up to a low murmur, in case anyone wanted to catch the morning news.

"You know," V-man said to no one in particular, although most of the guys at the bar listened whenever he spoke, just to see what might come out of his mouth. "Between Michigan, Ohio, and Pennsylvania, there must be at least three million deer hunters."

"What's your point?" AC asked.

"That could be an army all by itself. All those deer hunters could be their own militia, they are trained with weapons, they are woodsmen, and they know the local terrain, if only they had someone to lead them."

AC raised his eyebrows and shared a look with Big Mike and Brenda, "Did you have someone in mind?"

V-man caught the look among them and smiled as he shrugged but was thinking about what Patton had said. "I would be proud to lead you wonderful guys into battle, anytime, anywhere."

"Hey, how's that reunion coming along?" AC asked.

V-man shrugged. The search for Valenzuela hadn't been very productive, but he hadn't expected much on his first try, anyway. He wouldn't give up. More importantly, he had seen one of the guys from Valenzuela's neighborhood skulking around the streets near the bar the night before. He was doing a respectable job of keeping himself hidden and unobtrusive, but V-man's sharp eyes didn't miss much. He let the guy watch without disturbing him or letting on that he had been discovered. Hopefully, he would come around to meeting up with V-man on his own time.

"Some of these guys are easy to find. Ready to relive the glory days of fighting for our country. Others, you know, they want to bury those memories as deep as they can." V-man shook his head and took another sip of his coffee.

"If anyone can get them to a reunion, you can," AC said, before turning to wipe down a part of the counter recently vacated by a customer. "I think . . ." He was cut off by the ringing of the bell over the bar door and the loud booming voice of the man who stepped inside.

"I have you now, Able." The voice came from a stocky, muscled black police officer. He stepped inside, waving a piece of paper in the air.

AC's face transformed into a grim mask, without betraying any emotions. He folded his arms over his large chest. "Forrest," he said in a near growl. "Don't look so glum."

Forrest Williams was the chief of police for the entire city of Detroit. It was a difficult and largely thankless job, managing the large police force within the confines of budget cuts, all with the expectation of cleaning up the gangs, drugs, and violent crimes. He would deserve respect and sympathy if it wasn't for his vendetta against AC. "You knew this day would come eventually. A man like you can't stay on the right side of the law forever."

"What bullshit you wastin' my time with today, officer?" He said "officer" like it was a bad word.

"I got a call from the health office this morning." Forrest paused for dramatic effect. "Looks like you haven't been keeping up with the regulations. How 'bout you grab me a cup of coffee?"

AC kept his arms folded across his chest for a long moment before finally pouring a cup of coffee and sliding it down the bar toward the chief.

"Isn't this beneath your pay grade, Williams?" V-man asked. "With all the shit in this city, why are you doing the health inspector's job? Give him a ticket and move on."

"V-man, I have nothing but respect for you. I know the work you do for the community, but I don't know why you associate yourself with trash the likes of Able Cane here. He ain't worth the air he breaths." He took a slow sip of the coffee before making a face at the bitterness and sliding it aside.

"Chief Williams, I have nothing but respect for the force, putting yourself in the line of fire day in and day out, but you have to stop with this petty bullshit." V-man shook his head.

"That is where you are wrong, V-man. This isn't a simple ticket. I've got the authority to bring your buddy here in and charge him, maybe even close down the restaurant," Forrest claimed, waving the paper.

"What?" AC asked, moving around the bar in a smooth, aggressive movement. "Let me see that shit!"

"Not so fast. I gotta read you your rights," Forrest said, clearly enjoying the moment. "You have the right to remain silent," he began as he unclipped the handcuffs on his belt.

"I also have a right to know the charges," AC said.

Forrest ignored him and continued reading the Miranda rights. This wasn't the first time that V-man had to watch Forrest take AC in on trumped-up charges. Their contentious relationship went back to high school football. Each man had played for rival high school teams, which developed their initial competition. Every game became an excuse to trash talk and try to show the other man up. Things got especially complicated when Forrest started dating AC's sister, the one who ended up dead a few years ago. AC went through the roof when Chloe tried to bring Forrest home for a family dinner. AC, Chloe, Forrest, and their mom sat around the table in a tense silence as AC and Forrest kept glaring eyes on each other. At the time, Forrest was new to the force after recently graduating from the academy.

"Not sure why you couldn't have found a girl from your own neighborhood," AC said, breaking the silence.

"Don't start," Chloe said.

"I can date any girl I want," Forrest said.

"Not my sister," AC shouted, as he pushed back his chair with a loud scrape against the hardwood floor, so he could stand.

"Don't you tell her what she can and can't do. She is her own person, boy," Forrest said in his best condescending cop tone.

"Boy? Who are you calling boy?" AC said. Both men were shouting at this point. "I show you, boy."

"You threatening me?" Forrest said.

"Both of you sit down and stop this nonsense," AC's mom said.

"Perhaps we should take this outside?" AC said.

"Gladly," Forrest said.

After they had stepped outside, things escalated quickly. AC couldn't remember who had thrown the first punch, but it ended with him being dragged away by the police. The other officers didn't look too kindly on AC laying out one of their fellow uniforms. They charged him with assault and set an unreasonable bail before setting him free. For his part, Forrest didn't like the disgrace it brought him to have mostly lost the fight, so while his vendetta was strong before, he redoubled his efforts from that point on to bring AC down.

V-man saw the jealousy in Forrest's eyes every time he considered AC's success with the bar. It wasn't a far leap to imagine that's what brought Forrest down to the bar today, waving his paperwork and reading AC his rights.

Forrest had managed to free the handcuffs and was stepping closer to AC. "Don't give me any trouble now. That will only make it worse for you, boy."

AC slammed his fist onto the bar's countertop. "Don't call me boy."

While Forrest was distracted, V-man hopped off his high stool and sauntered casually up beside him and plucked the documents out of his hand.

"Hey, that is official police paperwork. You can't just take it," Forrest bellowed.

V-man ignored him, walking back to his seat as he unfolded the papers. He read through them quickly. They listed three prior unmitigated health code violations, which would be the basis for his arrest. It claimed that the health code official had reasonable cause to believe that AC violated and continually violated health codes and was therefore subject to arrest without warrant. V-man shook his head. Clearly, Forrest had the health department in his back pocket.

As he read through the violations, two were from before AC had taken ownership. The third, when a walk-in refrigerator was not kept at a cool-enough temperature, was when the inspector had come during a large blackout in the heat of the summer. They were bullshit charges. Forrest had no chance of detaining AC and probably wouldn't even be able to get a bail set for his release. When V-man looked up, Forrest was already motioning for AC to walk around the bar. AC hesitantly complied. When he made it to the other side of the bar, Forrest bent one of his arms behind his back and tightened one side of the cuffs around his wrist.

"Listen, Chief Williams," V-man said, hopping off his stool again. "You have the city's best interest at heart. You know that, I know that, and even AC knows it deep down, but you have to think rationally. These charges aren't going to last as long as it takes you to drive down to the station. As the chief, you have a reputation to consider. If you keep bringing AC down just to let him go, your men will lose their trust and faith in you. Best to let him go now, save face, and come back when you have something real. If he is as depraved as you imagine, then you will surely find something soon enough. Besides, you don't like my Jewish lawyers."

V-man had walked up to Forrest, so their faces were only inches apart. Forrest's dark brown eyes held a rage that clouded everything he felt, but V-man knew he hadn't gotten to be chief of police through his irrational anger. He got there through hard work, discipline, and skill. Without a word, he reached into his pocket for a key to the cuffs. The metal scraped into the keyhole and clicked open the handcuffs. When they came free, AC rubbed his wrists and turned around to stare at Forrest, who turned without a word and left the bar. The gaze he shot them when he left was a clear message that he would be back.

AC stepped behind the bar and cracked open a Pabst Blue Ribbon. When he saw V-man's expression, he shrugged and said, "It's five o'clock somewhere."

V-man sat back down in his seat, happy that AC had been saved the headache of going through the motions of being charged back at the police station. From the corner of his eye, he saw AC pull the chief's empty coffee cup down off the bar and wrap it in a clean napkin before putting it aside. The behavior was strange, but he wasn't in the habit of questioning his friend's motives.

He looked at the analog clock that hung on the wall behind the bar, wondering if he could have a beer, too, but since it was before noon, he figured he'd better abstain for the time being. Despite being the permanent caretaker of his friends, he had a day job to get to. He turned to go when the TV caught his attention. A large crowd had gathered outside of the courthouse where the "underwear bomber" was going on trial. It seemed like a lifetime ago that the terrorist made headlines with his botched attempt to blow up a plane with a bomb in his skivvies. Since then, there had been more attacks than he could count. He felt almost a personal responsibility whenever his country was attacked. He may have left the Army decades ago, but he never stopped fighting.

Watching the crowd gathered behind the reporter, a new suspicion developed. The young blond reporter spoke into her microphone as people behind her tried to shout their own opinion on the upcoming sentencing of the terrorist. She was in the process of describing the anticipated turnout of demonstrators on the day of the trial. If the crowd that had already gathered was any indication, V-man had no doubt it would be huge. He didn't trust it.

CHAPTER TEN

V-MAN STEPPED INTO THE UNSEASONABLY HOT SUN
that filled his backyard with golden early evening light. The smell of pro-
pane, coals, and meat filled his nose. Not for the first time, he was glad
he had gotten a dual-style grill. Different meats called for different types
of cooking methods, something that his wife just didn't understand, but
it was something he had to teach his children.

All of his neighbors had gathered for an impromptu barbecue to
enjoy the nice weather and good company. Almost everyone he knew
was there, save Big Mike and AC, who spent most of their time keeping
the bar up and running. The backyard behind his small ranch-style
home wasn't large, but it suited him just fine with some fold-out tables
and chairs and a sprinkler for the local kids.

Through the crowd, V-man caught sight of Amesh's new friend. He
paused. He always stuck to the philosophy of "the more, the merrier,"
but in this instance, the addition put him on high alert. The friend
looked mostly the same, although dressed more casually in American
style jeans and T-shirt, but his nose looked swollen and bruised as if
he had gotten into a bad fight. Moving through the crowd was a slow
process, as everyone who saw him had to stop and say hello. When he

finally made it to his destination, he was standing beside Amesh, but his friend had moved on to another conversation.

"You brought your house guest?" he asked, too straightforward for small talk.

Amesh looked around briefly before catching on to what V-man was referring to. "Oh yeah, I didn't think you would mind. I am sorry. Should I have asked you first?"

"No, no, it wasn't an accusation. How has he been?" he asked.

"Good, good. I think he is finally starting to settle in," Amesh said with a laugh.

"I sure hope so," V-man said, not sharing in the amusement. "What happened to his nose?"

"Oh, he said a couple of thugs tried to rob him."

"Is that so?"

It was certainly possible that Rahim had run into some troubled folks, but he would have had to specifically put himself in a bad neighborhood. Detroit had a reputation for being a hotbed of crime, gangs, and violence, but that wasn't entirely accurate. The crime around V-man and Amesh's neighborhood was almost nonexistent. They lived in a family-oriented part of town filled with rowhomes and single-family houses with a nearby park.

"It really is a shame. I wish that he hadn't had a negative experience while visiting here," Amesh said, shaking his head. "I want him to have a good impression of the States, after all."

"Why is he visiting?" V-man asked.

"He reached out to me a while back and said that he wanted to see America. "It is easier for people from my country to get visas to the States if they already know someone here."

"How do you two know each other?"

"We grew up in the same neighborhood back in Iraq. It is customary to host guests whenever possible," Amesh said. "It really was no trouble for us at all. We have the extra room, and he has been great with Jasim. I have seen more of Jasim in the past few weeks than I think I have in the past year."

"It must be nice to have more time with him. I sure wish I had that with my boys. How come he is coming around so much?"

Amesh shrugged. "They just get along really well. Rahim seems to like him."

The red flag that had initially flashed through V-man's mind when he saw Rahim at the party turned into a blaring siren that he couldn't ignore. V-man didn't know Jasim well enough to form an opinion on how vulnerable he might be to recruitment from a terrorist cell, but the time he was spending with Rahim worried him.

"How well do you know Rahim?" V-man asked.

Amesh looked up to the sky in thought. "Not very well, I suppose. Like I said, we grew up in the same neighborhood. He was always a good kid when we were in school, but I have been here since college, so it has been a long time since we have spent any real time together. He has been a very nice guest, though. Why so many questions?" Amesh looked at V-man with a serious expression.

"Just like to know who is coming and going in the neighborhood. Listen, don't hesitate to give me a call if you need anything, and keep an eye on that boy of yours," V-man said with a nod of his head. He left Amesh looking puzzled, but it wasn't unusual for a conversation with V-man to leave the participants scratching their heads in confusion.

V-man found his son near the grill, bringing a proud smile to his face. It was a rite of passage, taking over the barbecue at these functions. He put a hand on Luca's back.

"How's it going?" V-man asked, looking over his shoulder.

"Not bad," Luca said, wiping away the sweat that was forming on his brow with his sleeve.

"Not overcooking that meat, are you?" he said skeptically. The grill was filled with burgers, homemade Italian sausage, and steaks.

"Well, the first batch got a little overdone. Do you know if the temperature on your grill is very accurate?"

"It is a poor cook who blames the equipment, son," V-man said with a shake of his head and a smile. "Have I taught you nothing?"

"I guess not. I blame you mostly for the overdone meat today," Luca said, nudging his father in the ribs.

"I came over to ask you about your friend, not give you shit about the meat, although clearly, you needed some supervision. Amesh said Jasim was spending a lot of time with Rahim lately."

"Not this again. You and your crazy paranoia. What are you on about now?"

"If you had seen what I have seen in my life, you wouldn't be so quick to dismiss my concerns," V-man said. "Tell me about your friend. I haven't spent any time with him since you guys were in high school."

"There isn't much to tell. He lost his job a few months ago and has been struggling to find a new one. I know that he still has a lot of debt from his college bills, but his dad is helping him pay rent and keep him on his feet for the time being," Luca said with a shrug.

"How has he been handling the job loss?"

"Fine, Dad. He has been totally fine, even happy. He spends some time each day looking for a new job, and he hangs out with friends."

"What does he do in his free time?"

"Not like I watch him all the time, but he does normal stuff. He watches movies and plays video games."

"Does he spend a lot of time online?" V-man asked.

"I guess, no more than the rest of us."

"What does he do when he is hanging out with Rahim?"

"I don't really know. I have never gone along with them. He enjoys hanging out with him, and they hang out a lot. Since Rahim got here, I hardly see Jasim anymore. It kinda sucks, but when Rahim leaves, I am sure I will get my friend back."

"What do you mean?"

"Just that he is busy a lot. Normally when one of us meets someone new, whether it is a girl or just a new friend, we introduce them to each other. He did that at first with Rahim, but then he stopped inviting me along. When I question him about it, he said that he likes having someone around who understands him."

"Does he have any hobbies or interests that keep him busy?"

"Not really. When he is home he just kind of hangs out in front of the TV or on his computer."

"I am worried about your friend."

"Why? I'm not. We have been friends forever, I am not worried about the friendship."

"It's not necessarily the friendship." V-man paused, trying to find the right words, so his son would listen to him without blowing him off. "I am worried that Rahim isn't a great influence. It sounds like Jasim is in a vulnerable place after losing his job. He doesn't have any hobbies outside of hanging out at home. He may be soul-searching for an identity or a way to feel valuable. Rahim may provide him with just that."

"I don't even know what you are talking about, Dad," Luca said shaking his head in the dismissive way that only sons can do.

"Many soldiers are led to faulty ideas of war by knowing too much about too little," V-man said, quoting Patton.

"You aren't making any sense. Who is being led to war?"

"The point is, Luca, that any young man can be led to war on false ideas when those false ideas are the only information they are getting, and Rahim seems like just the type of person to spread that kind of over-blown radical rhetoric."

"You are being really racist, Dad."

V-man sighed and touched Luca's shoulder. "Son, not everyone is a good person. Sometimes bad people fit into our stereotypes. Tiptoeing around that fact doesn't make it go away. Nor does pointing it out make me a racist." This wasn't the first time V-man had to explain this to his son. "Jasim's friend has some deep-seated anger, and some piss-poor views of America. I worry that Jasim doesn't have the wherewithal to stand firm against it."

"I wouldn't read that much into this," Luca said, shrugging again. "It's no big deal."

"Stay vigilant, son." V-man walked back into the crowd to socialize. He kept an eye trained on Rahim, who spent most of the party hanging around Jasim. Whenever someone else approached the pair, Rahim would slip away with a knowing look toward Jasim, who would smile politely before cutting the conversation short to return to Rahim. When they spoke together, they bent their heads close conspiratorially, with Jasim nodding often.

Rahim pushed open his car door onto the street on the East Side of Detroit. A day earlier, he had been just a block or two south, trying to lure that nosey bitch into the abandoned school. He had spent each day since explaining how he had hurt his nose and imagining the slow and painful death of the border patrol girl. At least one good thing had come of the unfortunate encounter. He had come across the severely depressed and run-down neighborhood.

The neighborhood around him was visibly different from the one that he stayed in. For every two houses that looked lived in, there was at least one other that had boarded-up windows, graffiti, and a crumbling façade. Large groups of teenagers hung out on the corners. As he walked, his feet kicked up trash that littered the streets. He saw entire lots with demolished buildings left as nothing more than piles of rubble. The businesses looked like they were barely hanging on, while others were just vacant storefronts.

He kept his eyes sharp to prevent the story he told about his nose coming true. He also had to keep a careful watch in order to find the opportunity he was looking for. His initial recruiting had gone quickly. As soon as he arrived, he met with contacts that had been prearranged. Then he picked up a few more guys on his own. They had big plans, though, and he didn't want to risk being undermanned. As much as he wanted to dismiss the little girl on his trail, he also couldn't risk the plan going south.

He had a natural sense for the types of guys who would join his mission. Guys like Amesh's friend, who everyone called V-man, which Rahim thought it was a stupid nickname, was not the type of guy he was looking for. Even his son would mean bad news. It only took one conversation for him to assess an individual's mindset and potential willingness. The neighborhood he walked through now was very promising for the types of guys he was looking for. Tough, ruthless, poor, and with nothing to lose. The key, he had quickly learned, was in finding someone alone.

Most of the guys hanging around stood in groups. Approaching them with their friends, they would feel too confident. He kept walking. He came to the corner of Mack and Chalmers and paused, looking down the desolate streets. A young man walked from the gas station, crossing the four-lane highway as cars sped through, until he made it to the sidewalk beside Rahim. He barely acknowledged Rahim standing there except to give him a sideways glare when he held his gaze too long.

Rahim let the boy pass before he turned on his heels and jogged to catch up. The kid stopped walking and stood in a defensive posture when he realized he was being followed.

"What's your problem?" he asked angrily.

"Hey, hey, no problem," Rahim said as he held up his hands. "I just need a little help."

"I ain't ya' mama. Go find help somewhere else." He looked at Rahim with eyes that held a wealth of troubled experiences for someone so young.

Rahim chuckled at the vaguely threatening stance the young man had taken. He imagined that this boy's life up until this point had probably consisted of one heartbreak after the next. The world had turned its back on him, and he was ready for a fight.

"What the hell you laughing at, big man?" the boy said, stopping within an inch of Rahim's face.

"You are exactly the kind of person I am looking for."

"And what kinda person that be? Someone who's gonna kick yo ass?"

"Someone looking for an opportunity," Rahim said calmly.

"What the hell you talkin' about, son?"

"Look around you." Rahim waved his hand across the empty store fronts. "You think there are opportunities for you here?"

"Shit, there ain't no opportunities for me anywhere. I make my own opportunities."

"Then don't squander the one in front of you,"

"What the fuck you talkin' about, squanderin'?"

"I am offering you the opportunity to get out of this ghetto."

"Oh yeah? And how you gonna do that? Ain't nobody get out of this town."

"That's because no one is willing to fight the system that holds them down."

"Bullshit, we fight the system every day."

"Not well," Rahim said.

"Fuck you, man," the kid said, turning to walk away.

"Look at me," Rahim said, spreading his arms out wide. He pulled his iPhone out of his pocket and jangled his expensive watch. "I have new clothes, new shoes, and the latest tech. I have everything I want."

"I could just take that shit from you," the boy said, but Rahim could tell his bravado was weakening.

"I guess you could, but this stuff will go out of style. What happens when you want something new? You could be something more than a low-life thug, my friend. You could travel the world; you could fight for a purpose and be a hero instead of trying to scrape enough pennies together for some food and drugs."

At this, the kid stepped back and screwed up his face in confusion and suspicion. His head tilted to the side. "Who the fuck wants to be a hero? What the fuck is you talkin' about?"

"This way of life is unfair. You shouldn't have to live like this. With me, you can wage war on the people at the top. You can live in honor and glory while bringing equality and justice to the world," Rahim said.

Realization finally flashed over the kid's face, "You some kind of terrorist or some shit?"

"No, not a terrorist, a freedom fighter. Saving people like you from the oppression your fellow countrymen place on you. Why do they get to live in luxury while you struggle every single day?"

"This is fucking, America, son. Don't bring your jihadist bullshit up in my 'hood. Trying to destroy the country? Fuck that," he shouted. He turned and ran before Rahim could say anything else.

He reached a larger group of young men on the opposite corner, who had been lounging casually until the kid started talking to them and gesturing toward Rahim. Each one looked up in turn with a burning hatred in their eyes. Rahim took the hint and ran for his car. As soon as his feet started beating against the pavement in his imported leather shoes, the group of guys took off after him with shouts of rage. With his heart trying to beat through his chest, he managed to slam his car door shut just as the guys reached him. They punched their fists against the metal and shook the car, screaming as he turned the key in the ignition. The guys had surrounded him, but he pressed his foot down on the gas, and they jumped out of the way. In the rearview mirror, he watched them run a few steps after him, but he didn't think he had to worry about them calling the cops. He had violated the rules of the street. The locals grew up in the 'hood, and they well knew the situation. They didn't need this outsider coming in and "preaching" to them. Rahim was fortunate to escape when he did.

When he was closer to a more familiar and safer neighborhood, he pulled his cell out of his pocket. "Jasim," Rahim said, when he heard a voice say hello. "The plan didn't work."

"Rahim? What plan?" It wasn't Jasim on the other end of the line. It was Amesh.

"Oh hey, Amesh," Rahim said, quickly changing his tone to the light and friendly one he used around everyone else. "I thought I was calling Jasim's cell."

"You were, but he left it lying in the kitchen. When I saw your number, I thought I would answer, so it didn't go to voicemail. What plan didn't work?" Amesh asked.

"I was trying to get us free tickets to the movie with an old discount card I found, but it didn't work. The guys at the theater knew it was expired. Is Jasim there?"

"Oh," Amesh said with suspicion in his tone. "I think so. Is everything all right?"

"Yeah, man, no worries. We will just have to buy our tickets to the movies," Rahim said with a laugh.

"Okay, I will get Jasim," he said before setting the phone down.

After a moment's pause, a new voice came on the line. "Hello?"

"Jasim, you cannot leave your phone unattended. Ever."

"I am sorry. It won't happen again," Jasim said.

"Good. Our plan didn't work. These thugs think they are too good for our plan. We are better off anyway, though. We don't want any loose cannons screwing us up. Only the truly faithful deserve eternal salvation by participating in God's work. Are you taking care of that backpack I gave you?"

"Yes," Jasim said enthusiastically. "I haven't let it out of my sight."

"Good, you will be rewarded well. The plan is set then. I will contact the others. Our rendezvous will be in two days. You will set the explosives, then we will set up a perimeter and take out anyone who escapes the bomb. From there we will get on the trucks and go back to Canada."

"Got it." Jasim's voice held a quiver that could indicate both excitement and nervous hesitation.

"Jasim, my brother, you mustn't let yourself become clouded by doubts sowed by the opposition. They will try to buy you with their lavish comforts and godless ways, all while seeking to destroy everything we are. They hate us. They will stop at nothing to destroy us. Look at yourself. Why did you lose your job while everyone around you got to keep theirs? It isn't a coincidence. With me, you are part of something so much more. You are a hero to your people, not some nameless face in a corporation bent on filling the pockets of American bankers and lawmakers who will only further our own desolation. This American way is not for us."

"I understand," Jasim said more firmly. "I will not fail you."

"Good. I will see you in two days. There are others who will join us."

CHAPTER ELEVEN

V-MAN SIPPED HIS COFFEE SLOWLY. HE HADN'T slept well the night before. Despite enjoying the barbecue, he kept seeing Rahim's face when he first met him as he sneered and complained about Americans. Something wasn't right. He knew that without a doubt, but he couldn't exactly call the cops because someone didn't like America. Nonetheless, he couldn't sit around doing nothing, waiting for Rahim to start killing people. He needed more information about Rahim and Jasim. Where they went together, what kinds of things they did, and if Rahim had given Jasim any hints about a plan.

His best bet revolved around Jasim, and to get to Jasim, he needed Luca on board. V-man stared off into space as he contemplated his next move. Around him, the bar was mostly empty. The only sounds came from the muffled news coming from the TV and the clanking of dishes in the back where Jerome cleaned dishes for some extra cash. Last V-man had heard, Jerome and Homer had almost gotten into a fist fight the night before while V-man was hosting his barbecue. He worried about those kids. If Jerome didn't get his shit together soon, he would wind up on the same path as his mother. Watching him act like a fool was killing AC.

Whenever AC would get tough and rein him in, Jerome would act out more. When he gave him some space and left him to his own devices, he would stay up partying and show up late for work. It was going to take everything AC had to keep that young man's life on the straight and narrow. V-man, who for the most part had advice for everyone in every situation, didn't know what to tell him to do with Jerome. This latest scuffle was just another reminder of what happened to his mother.

"Deep in thought today, V?" Brenda asked as she wiped down the counter.

Much like V-man, she had a tendency to take care of everyone at the bar. V-man looked up from his coffee. "I tell ya, Brenda, nothin's easy anymore."

"Was it ever?" she asked with a smile.

"I don't know. Back when I was a kid, we would listen to Motown, race our hot rods, and not bother with all the drama. I miss those days."

"Don't we all," she said. "Although, didn't you go into the war pretty soon after?"

"I did, but even that seems simpler in retrospect. We went there to do a job, and we did it well. Now you got terrorists everywhere trying to divide us."

"Don't let it get you down, Hun." She moved on to cleaning tables, leaving V-man alone with his thoughts again.

Before he could even take another sip of coffee, he felt his phone buzz in his pocket. When he fished it out, the caller ID said Amesh. An uncomfortable knot formed in the pit of the stomach. It couldn't have been good news.

"V-man here," he said into the phone.

"V-man, it is Amesh." His tone sounded worried, almost frantic.

"What's happened?" V-man asked, skipping pleasantries.

"I don't want you to think that I have gone crazy, but I am worried about Jasim," Amesh said in his thick Middle Eastern accent. V-man didn't respond, waiting for Amesh to continue. "Last night, Jasim's phone rang. When I saw that it was Rahim, I picked up. Rahim thought I was Jasim, and he was talking about a plan."

"What kind of plan?"

"I don't know. I am sure it is nothing, but after our conversation yesterday, I started getting worried. I wouldn't want Jasim involved in anything," Amesh said.

"What exactly did he say?"

"He said the plan didn't work out. When he found out it was me, his tone changed."

"Amesh, this isn't something to mess around with. You have to contact the police immediately and tell them your suspicions," V-man said adamantly.

"What if it is nothing? I don't want to get Jasim in trouble. I know how people are. They get very nervous about Middle Easterners. I don't want anyone overreacting," Amesh said.

"If Jasim is innocent, then the police will find that out pretty quickly. He might be inconvenienced for a day. The alternative is much, much worse for everyone,"

"How do you mean? What do you think the plan was?" Amesh said warily.

"I know that Rahim is your guest, but I have been worried about him since the second I met him. I don't know what their plans may have been, but I know that something isn't right. If Rahim is trying to pull Jasim into some sort of ISIS terrorist plot, then you will never see Jasim again. This is a rare opportunity to prevent something before anything happens to Jasim,"

"I don't know, V-man. You seem so sure something underhanded is going on, but I don't know if Jasim or Rahim would ever forgive me if I turned them in as suspected terrorists. Rahim would lose his travel visa, and Jasim might have difficulty getting a job. I feel like I need more to go on than a strange phone call."

V-man shook his head and rubbed his temple with his free hand. The conversation was painfully frustrating. "Amesh, you don't want to be that guy," he said finally.

"What guy?"

"That guy that we hear about on the news. That guy that thought maybe something was up but didn't say anything. You don't want Jasim to be a victim of your complacency. Better alive and angry than dead." He let the words hang in the air. Silence came from the other end of the line.

"I suppose you are right. I will stop by the police station today before work," Amesh said.

"Let me know what they say."

"I will. And thank you, V-man."

Amesh walked up the steps of the historic building, repeating V-man's words to himself. His feet felt like lead, climbing the steps to turn in his own son. With each step upon the beige-colored cement, his hesitation and dread grew.

As he pulled open the front door of the police station, to the whir-ring sound of a window unit air conditioner, he was struck by a thought that he hadn't had before. What if Jasim was involved in some sort of terrorist plot? His blood ran cold at the thought. Would they spare him since he was young? Would they be lenient since the plot wasn't carried out? Would he be sentenced just as harshly as those who had coerced him? The thoughts terrified him and almost made him turn back. He paused just inside the door. The worst-case scenario to all of his unanswered questions played out in his mind. Finally, he came to the worst-case scenario if he didn't tell the police about his suspicions, and V-man's words replayed again. "Better alive and angry than dead."

After everything he had sacrificed to get to find success in America, so his children could have a good life, he couldn't throw it all away because he was worried Jasim would be mad. With renewed vigor, Amesh stepped forward. The police station was always busy in a city like Detroit. Civilians and officers came and went with what seemed important purpose, while other waited in chairs lined up along the side of the room. In front of him was a large reception desk. He stepped up to it and cleared his throat while his heart beat feverishly and his palm sweat nervously.

The woman at the desk looked up briefly before bringing her eyes back to the computer screen in front of her. "Can I help you?" she asked.

"Um, yes, I think so, I want to speak to an officer, please," he said.

"What officer?" she asked. Her name tag read "Joan."

"I didn't have a particular one in mind. I just wanted to report something."

"What does it pertain to?"

"Well, um, I don't really know, I just, it might be nothing. I just wanted to speak to any officer, I guess." Amesh cringed at how nervous he must have sounded.

"Please have a seat, sir, I will have an officer come speak to you."

"Thank you," he said bowing his head slightly. He took a seat in one of the uncomfortable wooden chairs that looked about as old as the building itself. After what felt like far too long fretting in the waiting area, an officer came out from the back hallway and approached Amesh.

"Hi there," he said, in what he probably intended to be a polite tone, but instead came out as bored or indifferent. "Joan said you needed to talk to an officer. Why don't you follow me back to one of the offices?"

The officer, who introduced himself as Jim MacNamara, led him back to an open room with a lot of desks spread throughout. Jim sat down behind one and motioned for Amesh to sit on the other side.

"What brings you in?" he asked, pulling up a program on his laptop to take a report.

"Well, now that I am sitting here, I am not sure what to say," Amesh began.

"Why don't you give it a try?" the officer said, cutting him off impatiently.

"I have had a house guest for the past week. He is visiting from the Middle East. He has been a wonderful guest, really. He picks up after himself. He is polite and helpful, and my son has really taken a liking to him. Recently, I heard my guest talking about a plan, and it made me a little nervous. I just wanted to make sure everything is on the up and up."

The officer looked up at Amesh for the first time with a serious expression. "What kind of plan?" he asked slowly.

"That is the problem. I don't know, but his tone changed when he realized I was on the line. My son is a good boy. I just want to make sure he isn't making bad choices," Amesh said, suddenly feeling doubtful again.

"I am gonna call in the chief on this one," the guy said, before getting up and walking further into the building. He was back a few moments later, talking with the chief of police.

"Hello there. I am Chief Williams, nice to meet you," he said, holding out his hand to shake Amesh's.

"Nice to meet you, too. I am Amesh," he said shaking the chief's hand. The chief pulled up a seat alongside officer MacNamara.

"Jim here has been telling me that you are concerned about a plan you overheard," the chief said. Amesh relayed the story again in as much detail as he could remember. When he was done, the chief and the officer shared a look that Amesh couldn't discern. "Well, you are right. It isn't much to go on, but we will alert Homeland Security, and I will send an officer out to the house to check up on the boys. You did the right thing by telling us. We will hope that it is nothing, right?" he said with a friendly smile meant to ease Amesh's anxiety.

Amesh nodded, and the officers ushered him out. He had a sick feeling in his stomach, unsure if he had done the right thing or not.

The chief studied the small brownstone that was indistinct from any other house on the block, save for a few blooming flowers in a window box on the first-floor window that peeked their yellow blossoms out in the warm spring weather. He tugged on his belt, pulling his pants up over his oversized belly. He had been watching the house for no more than five minutes, but he guessed no one was home. After doing this for as many years as he had, his instincts were fine tuned.

"All right," he said to the gathered officers. "Let's go."

The officers broke into three groups. Three officers moved through the tight alley beside the house to the back door. Three more, including the chief, moved on the front door while the rest formed a watchful perimeter.

The chief rapped against the door with his knuckles. In his hand, he had written permission to enter the house from Amesh, who stood anxiously outside the perimeter. Forrest didn't have to wait for an answer, but he waited for a few breaths nonetheless. When no answer came, he gave the signal, and the police moved into the house. Heavy boots stomped through the hardwood floors. Officers quickly canvased the house before reconvening in the centralized first-floor hallway, all shaking their heads that they didn't find anyone home.

Not surprised by the findings, the chief stepped outside and waved Amesh over. He stepped tentatively through the line of officers before meeting Forrest on the front stoop.

"Which bedroom was he staying in?" the chief asked.

Amesh led him through the house until they came to a small guest room. The chief stepped in to find an undisturbed room without any personal effects or signs of life. The bed was neatly made with the corners tucked in, while the dresser, nightstand, and closet were void of anything that might belong to a guest.

"Did he always travel this light?" Forrest asked.

"No, he had a few suitcases, and I think a blue book bag. I don't know where he could have gone."

"Looks like he is missing to me," the chief said.

He walked out of the room to meet back up with his officers.

"I want to check out the kid's apartment," the chief said. He left Amesh wringing his hands on the sidewalk, more worried now than when everything had started.

The unmarked cruiser that belonged to the chief pulled up in front of an apartment complex. Along with a few other officers, he stepped up to the front door and pushed the button to Jasim's apartment.

"Can I help you?" a voice responded from the speaker grid.

"Chief Williams, Detroit police department. We are looking for Jasim Nazari."

The voice on the other end of the intercom hesitated. "Um, what is this about?"

"Police business. Is he home?"

"No," the voice said.

"May we come up?" the chief asked.

"Do you have a warrant?"

"No. We are hoping you can cooperate with us and answer a few questions without wasting any precious time in getting the paperwork."

The officers waited until finally, the door buzzed, and the lock clicked open. They climbed the stairs to the second story. The apartment building wasn't the worst that Forrest had ever seen, but it was clearly under-maintained. When they came to Jasim's apartment, the door was held open by Luca. The chief recognized him as the son of V-man.

"So, what is going on?" he asked. He had his cell phone in his hand, and it buzzed with a text message.

"Is that Jasim texting you now?"

Luca glanced at the phone. "No, I tried Jasim, but he hasn't written me back. This message is from my father."

"Where is Jasim?"

"I don't know. He has been out a lot lately," Luca said warily.

"Do you go with him when he goes out?"

"Not lately."

"Why's that?" the chief asked.

105

Luca shrugged.

"You mind if I take a quick peek in his room?"

"I am not sure about that," Luca said, hesitating.

"Boy, his father is worried about him, and after listening to his father, and seeing his new friend skip town, I am worried, too. If you care about your friend, you would want us to find him and make sure everything is all right."

"Wait, Mr. Nazari called you guys?"

"He sure did."

"Why?"

"Like I said, we are all worried about him."

Luca studied the chief's face, trying to gauge his sincerity. He finally stepped into the apartment and motioned for the officers to follow. "You aren't going to touch anything, are you?"

"No, I just want to take a look."

Luca opened Jasim's bedroom door, and the chief stepped inside. The room was in the opposite condition from the one at Amesh's house. The bed was disheveled and unmade without even a blanket on it. The dresser's drawers were pulled open with clothes spilling out.

"Is this how he normally keeps his room?" the chief asked.

"No, I have never seen it like this." For the first time, Luca was genuinely worried for his friend.

"Aside from the mess, does it look like anything is missing?"

Luca stepped further into the room and scrutinized the disarray. "His laptop isn't here," he said, pulling open the closet. "He normally has a duffle bag of racketball gear in here, but that has all been dumped, and the bag is missing. I never really took stock of all his stuff, though."

The chief nodded in thought.

"What does it mean?" Luca asked.

"It means I think your friend and his friend are gone, but we may have bigger concerns than that." The chief brushed past Luca to address his men. "Get Homeland on the line again. Tell them our perps are AWOL. Get an alert out to all of our guys with the descriptions."

Luca was left standing in his friend's room with his stomach turning. He texted his friend again but didn't receive a response.

CHAPTER TWELVE

THE FAINT SOUND OF A SCREEN DOOR SQUEEZING
shut sounded over the hum of Anna's car engine, pulling her attention
up in time to watch Rahim hurry down the steps of the brownstone, lug-
ging a large duffle bag behind him. He popped the trunk of his Honda
and loaded the bag inside before turning on his heels to go back into the
house, taking the steps two at a time. Anna's heart rate picked up as the
screen door slammed again, and Rahim reemerged with his arms loaded
with another heavy bag. She should have learned her lesson the last time
she tried to follow him, but it wasn't part of her programming to give up.
A burning desire to put an end to his plan drove her to continue despite
the obvious risks. Admittedly, some small part of her motivation was to
prove everyone wrong, much like when she hunted with her brothers.
Regardless of the reasoning, it had led her to sitting in her idling car,
watching a suspected terrorist anxiously packing all of his belongings.

He held his shoulders in an anxious hunch while his head shifted
back and forth, constantly checking his surroundings. What he was
checking for, she wasn't sure. Maybe he was ready to carry out his plan,
or perhaps he simply was paranoid about being caught. Either way, his
behavior made it clear that he wasn't planning on returning to this
brownstone. The trunk slammed closed once he had finished making

trips inside, and he climbed into the driver's seat before peeling out of his spot.

As she pulled out a few car lengths behind him, flashing red and blue police lights filled her rearview mirror. Finally, the police were getting involved. Again, the voice of reason in the back of her mind pleaded with her to turn around, tell the police what she knew and never think of Rahim again. But she didn't listen. She had let him through the border. He was her responsibility, and she meant to see it through.

They wound through the city streets that, despite her more frequent visits, were mostly unfamiliar to her. Each time it looked like they were slowing to a stop, he proceeded forward, sometimes changing directions. She started suspecting that he had no real destination at all. If he stopped, she wouldn't get out of the car. She wasn't going to be lured into a trap alone. She didn't have to worry long about that possibility because after about thirty-five minutes he chose a direction. He turned onto I-94 east toward her home. In a moment of paranoia, Anna imagined Rahim had discovered where she lived with her family outside of Saint Clair and was heading that way to silence her. She took a deep breath. *I won't let that happen,* she thought. Despite being out of her element the last time they met, she had prepared ahead for this time. She carried her government-issued hand gun in a holster strapped to her chest, her hunting knife strapped to her thigh, and of course, she had her rifle in the back. The rifle was, of course, her weapon of choice, but the other weapons allowed her flexibility in fighting style, depending on the situation. In hand-to-hand combat, her training would kick in, just as well as her targeting skills.

The vibrating of her phone pulled her out of her thoughts. The cell lay on the passenger seat. The screen read Ivan Kazenko, with a smiling picture of her brother displayed beneath the name. Anna sighed. A new anxiety developed in the pit of her stomach. Her brothers had gotten increasingly suspicious, and she didn't want to have to lie about her whereabouts again. Since she had told them she was trailing a terrorist, she got almost hourly phone calls, checking in with where she was and what she was doing. During work hours, she didn't hesitate to answer because she had a ready-made excuse that would make her whole family feel better. If she didn't answer though, things would be worse when she got home.

With another sigh, she answered the phone, putting it on speaker, so her brother's voice filled the car.

"Anna, where are you?" he said, skipping the pleasantries.

"Just driving," Anna said, cursing herself for not coming up with a new alibi.

"Just driving? Where are you driving to or from?" he asked suspiciously.

"I went out to grab a bite to eat after work,"

"Another bite to eat?" Ivan said.

She heard a scuffle on the other end of the line before her dad's voice came through. "Anastasia Tatyana Kazenko. You stop lying to us. Tell us where you are right now." The anger and fear fought in his voice as he tried to remain calm.

"Dad, I don't want you to worry," she said, feeling an overwhelming guilt for deceiving her family.

"If you don't want us worrying, then you should tell us where you are and what you are doing."

"I was just grabbing a bite of food." Her voice had lost all its conviction.

"Anna, do not treat me like a fool. I have been in your position. Fighting for what I think is right while hiding from those around me. Why do you not trust me?"

"I have to do this, Dad. It is my fault this man is in the country, and I have to make it right. I have to make sure he doesn't hurt anyone."

"This isn't your fight. Let the authorities take care of it."

"The authorities don't move quickly enough. I have to do this."

"Then I will do it," her father said.

"No! I am not dragging all of you into this."

"Anna, that is what you don't understand. We are already in this. We have always been in this because you are in this. Where are you now?"

Anna remained silent for a long stretch of time, debating her options. If she told them, they would come. The thought of not being alone on this reckless chase was appealing, but her father wasn't a young man anymore, and her brothers had no formal training. "I am sorry, Daddy," she said quietly, before hanging up the phone. She stared ahead, blinking the tears out of her eyes. It was the right thing, she repeated over and over again, trying to convince herself.

Olek handed the phone back to Ivan, shaking his head. While he felt a burning anger that his daughter defied him, his worry consumed him. The three men sat on the old brown couches of their living room. The TV in front of them ran on mute. Tatyana, thankfully, had been outside working with the farm hands to finalize a shipment. Like her daughter, she wasn't delicate. She had seen plenty of hardships in her life, but if she knew about the danger her daughter was in, she would be frantic.

111

"What happened? What did she say?" Ivan said, looking at the blank screen of his phone.

"She is after the terrorist. She wouldn't tell me where," Olek said.

"We have to call her back; make her tell us,"

"She won't. She is too much like me." Olek shook his head. "This is my fault. I filled her head with stories of the Resistance, of fighting for justice. She won't stop until it is done."

"It isn't your fault."

"We have to do something," Pavlo said.

"What can we do? We don't even know where she is," Ivan said.

"We could call the police."

"No," Olek said. "We go to her ourselves."

He rose from the couch.

"How? We don't know where she is," Pavlo said. His voice rose with frustration as he stood to confront his father.

Olek looked in Pavlo's eyes, then at Ivan. "Follow me."

Without waiting to see if they followed, Olek walked through the front door and stepped down onto the gravel driveway.

"Dad?" Ivan was cut off by his father raising his hand to silence him. He sighed and trudged out the front door.

Olek made his way around the side of the house before turning toward the barn. His sons grudgingly followed, occasionally trying to get information out their dad, who remained tight-lipped. Olek pulled open the barn doors and stepped up to his locked office. Ivan's eyes grew wide as he shared a shocked look with Pavlo.

"You are letting us in?" Ivan asked.

"Yes," was all Olek said. His tone clearly communicated that he didn't like the prospect but had no choice.

"What is in there? How will it help Anna?" Pavlo said.

"You will see in a moment," Olek said, shaking his head. At times, he forgot that his boys were older than Anna. He fished the keys out of his pocket, unlocking the padlock, which came off with a loud thunk and landed in the dirt at his feet. The door creaked open, sounding like a tomb that had been sealed for centuries, even though Olek still visited his office every night.

When they stepped inside Ivan, and Pavlo gawked at the sight of it. The room was small, no larger than a galley-sized kitchen. Old technology lined three of the walls, boxy computer monitors, two-way radios, army-green headphones that could have been in a museum. It looked like a scene from a WWII movie.

"What is all of this, Dad?" Ivan said.

"Does it even work?" Pavlo asked.

"Yes, of course, it works." Olek flipped on a surge protector power cord, causing a low hum to resonate through the small space. One by one each of the screens flickered to life. He moved around the room, turning dials and flipping switches until the entire room vibrated with the power of electronics.

"Is this all from when you were in Russia?" Ivan asked.

"Yes. I have added some upgrades, though," Olek said, sitting in a wheeled office chair that allowed him to glide across the floor between screens and radios. Ivan and Pavlo were left standing awkwardly behind him since the room hadn't been designed with guests in mind. Olek's fingers flew across a keyboard as he typed. The screen closest to him flickered to life with a black-and-white picture of the interstate. In the center, a little dot blinked on and off, moving along the highway. "There," Olek said, touching his finger to the dot.

"You tagged her car?" Pavlo said in shock.

"Of course," Olek said dismissively, as if there was no other choice. "She is driving east on I-94, from Detroit to home."

The three men studied the blinking white dot on the screen as it moved slowly up the line that represented nterstate 94. All of them were familiar with the road, having traveled it countless times. What business Anna had on it was the mystery.

"I guess she is on her way home," Ivan said.

Olek shook his head. "I should have given you more training, Ivan. If your sister were simply on her way home, she would have said as much. We don't know what she is up to, but it is something—something dangerous."

The words settled around them like an uncomfortable blanket as they all pondered what to do about it. She was still a good forty-five minutes away. Neither one wanted to wait for Anna to decide on her own to give up. They knew her well enough to know that would never happen.

"Ivan, Pavlo, call your friends, Buddy and Jimmy. Tell Buddy to reach out to his father," Olek said as he stood, pulling a smaller monitor from a pile of electronics and flipping the switch on. Olek went directly to the rifle rack. He carefully picked up his rifle and examined it, grabbing extra loaded magazines. Ivan and Pavlo instinctively did the same as if this drill had been practiced many times. Ivan also texted Jimmy and Buddy.

Anna lost focus as the monotony of the drive wore on her. Her fingers flicked through the radio dial until an upbeat pop song blasted through the speaker. Then she occupied herself by singing along before she realized she no longer had eyes on the black Honda she was trailing. She had been driving for at least twenty minutes on the endless, uninterrupted expressway, easily keeping track of the Honda. After all, there weren't many places for it to hide. Her eyes shifted quickly over the long, unbroken stretch of highway in front of her, trying to find Rahim's car again. The road had suddenly become very crowded in the small space directly surrounding her Jeep Cherokee.

The road had three east- and west-bound lanes, with a few cars speeding through, but directly beside her car, four others had slowed traffic to box her in. To her right, in a red four-door, Japanese-made sedan, that must have been at least eight years old, she met the hard eyes of a Middle Eastern man. His piercing stare tried to bore a hole through her head. When she looked to the other side, she was met with the same thing. She turned her gaze forward to see the glaring red brake lights of a black SUV. Her sweaty hands slipped on the steering wheel as she tried to steady her rapid breathing.

Her foot tapped the brakes to prevent her front bumper from hitting the car in front of her. They were forcing her to slow down until she reached a near crawl of fifty-five miles per hour. Other cars zoomed past with blaring horns at the slow progress of the road block surrounding Anna. She shook her head in frustration at letting herself fall into another trap. What would her father say about her stupid mistake? Her anger helped calm the fear that tried to choke her.

Her mind worked through the possible scenarios, visualizing them play out. It was possible they simply wanted to keep her occupied while Rahim got away, although it seemed unlikely that he would let her get away again.

Regardless of their motives, she didn't have time for this. If Rahim was planning something, she had to stop it. She tightened her grip on the wheel and swerved her car to the right. The side of her Grand Cherokee came within an inch of the SUV as it veered to the right to avoid a collision. Without hesitation, her foot pressed on the gas, and she squeezed into the opening left by the dodging car. The green paint scraped along the rear bumper of the front car with a nails-on-chalkboard sound, while the right headlight shattered on the front bumper of the right-hand SUV. The driver had apparently realized his mistake and was trying to close the gap. Luckily for her, he hadn't realized in time.

She broke away from the men as her outdated car fought against its age to climb to eighty miles per hour. The engine roared louder than it should have but didn't let her down. Behind her, the sound of revving engines filled the highway as the four cars took up the chase. She wove through the slower-moving traffic as surprised motorists waved angry hand gestures out their window. Her car broke free into an open lane. When she glanced at the speedometer, her eyes grew large at the needle hovering above ninety-five miles per hour. She had a brief moment to feel proud of her old car for going so fast before she glimpsed a black SUV out of the corner of her eye. A quick look in the rearview mirror revealed the red sedan gaining ground on her bumper.

Shifting to the right lane, she cut off the black SUV, but inadvertently gave room for the red sedan to pull up beside her. Each of the four cars that had boxed her in encroached on her. She pushed the car harder until the speedometer needle quavered around one hundred. The wheel rattled almost imperceptibly beneath her fingers as if the wheels themselves might fly off if she went any faster. In the lane opposite the red sedan, she saw the fourth car that had originally been behind her, trying to gain momentum to box her in again. She swerved to the right this time, and her rear bumper clipped the SUV. What would normally have been a small force sent her car into a wild fishtail as she desperately clung to the wheel. Behind her, the SUV had spun through two lanes of traffic, creating a two or three-car pile-up of innocent drivers.

The steering wheel beneath her fingers finally seemed under control, although her nerves felt liked live wires sizzling beneath her skin. She kept her speed in the eighties while she tried to regain sights of the other cars in pursuit. She didn't have to wonder long because a heavy thud slammed into her rear passenger side, throwing her car spinning. When it came to a stop, her head slammed against the wheel. Black specks floated in her vision. As she tried to blink them away, she realized she was facing the wrong way on the highway, and her engine was silent.

Her fingers desperately turned the key in the ignition, getting a grinding, moaning sound. In front of her, two cars pulled to a stop. When the doors opened, the only thing between her and the AK 47 assault rifles was a thin pane of cracked windshield glass.

CHAPTER THIRTEEN

THE SOUR FEELING IN V-MAN'S STOMACH HADN'T dissipated since his call from Amesh. Work had moved slowly as he tried without success to focus on anything other than the unfolding crisis around him. He still had no solid evidence of a crisis, but he knew it nonetheless. Growing up in the rough streets of Detroit and fighting his way through Vietnam had developed a sixth sense for trouble. Half the time, it was trouble he ran toward rather than away from. In this instance, he couldn't do either. He drove through the crowded rush-hour jammed streets of downtown Detroit, planning on grabbing something to eat before heading home.

He found himself at an intersection, waiting for the light to turn green, when a small black car that looked a lot like Rahim's passed by, but it was the girl in the car behind it that gave him pause. He thought he knew most of the faces in his small neighborhood, but she was unfamiliar. It was the second or third time he had seen the green Jeep Cherokee driven by a young blonde woman lurking around the neighborhood. Something about her set alarm bells off in his head. Twice now, he had seen her in close proximity to Rahim. He prepared himself to turn the wheel to follow when his phone vibrated.

Dad, I need to talk to you ASAP. The urgent message came from Luca. With thoughts of the little blonde girl pushed out of his head by his concern for Luca, he sped down the back roads until he came to his son's apartment building. He debated calling his son but opted for just getting to his apartment instead. If there really was a problem, he couldn't fix it over the phone.

"What is it?" V-man asked, when his son ushered him inside.

"I am sure you know now that the police came by my place looking for Jasim. Do you really think we should be worried about him?"

"I didn't know the police came by, but yes, I do think we should worry about him. We have to find him."

"Shouldn't we leave that to the police?"

"Son, I thought you would know me better by now," V-man said. He walked through the small, messy apartment, keeping keen eyes out for anything relevant to Jasim's whereabouts. When he made his way back to Jasim's room, his eyebrows lifted. He rifled through the drawers briefly before picking up some dirty clothes on the floor. He rifled through the pockets of a few crumpled and inside-out jeans before coming away with a small slip of paper. He held it between his fingers triumphantly before unfolding it.

"He planning on doing a lot of gardening?" V-man asked with a raise of his eyebrows.

"What?" Luca asked.

"This receipt is from the garden center up on West Fort Street. Looks like he spent a good amount there. It isn't itemized, but I can only imagine one thing he might need. Typically, you can't buy a ton of fertilizer in one place anymore, but small places like that probably wouldn't think twice about it."

"No," Luca said shaking his head. "I don't believe it. Jasim wouldn't get mixed up in shit like that. He would never want to hurt anyone."

V-man put a hand on his son's shoulder. "We need to accept what comes our way, Luca. You can still care about your friend, but also accept he has been lured into some dark shit. I have to see what I can find out about this receipt, but most importantly, we have to find Jasim. Keep texting him, but do not meet him. Let me know if you hear anything."

V-man stepped into the Corner Bar, eliciting the stares of the patrons, including Jay, who sat at the bar taking tiny sips of his beer before wrinkling up his face.

"Not sure how you drink this stuff every day," Jay said as V-man approached. "Next time you are in DC, I am taking you on a tour of some microbreweries."

"That shit ain't for me. I am a simple man, Jay," V-man said, slapping him on the back, causing the beer to slosh around in the bottle. "What brings you back here?"

"I heard you were getting yourself into some trouble," he said. "I came up here to check on you."

V-man laughed taking a seat on the stool beside Jay as Brenda slid a beer in his direction. "I appreciate the thought, but I think you just came up here to be part of the action. Who told you and what did they say?"

"I got a text from a number I didn't recognize," Jay said, pulling his phone out of his pocket and scrolling through to find the text.

"Sounds sketchy," V-man said.

"You're telling me. The text might be from someone trying to mislead us, or it could be from a concerned friend. Either way, I figured you could use some help."

Jay held out his phone, so V-man could read the words on the screen: *Shit going down in Detroit. Keeping an eye on V-man.*

"What concerned friend would send an anonymous text instead of just tellin' us?" V-man asked.

Jay shrugged. "We did go visit Valenzuela recently; you think it could be him?"

"Could be. I thought I have seen his guys around town since we tried reachin' out. He hasn't made any overt gesture to make contact, though."

"Is it accurate?"

"What?"

"The text?"

V-man nodded. "Shit is going down, that is for sure. Worse than I had imagined."

"All right, what is it?"

"A friend of mine has a house guest, well more accurately, had a house guest who I am confident is a terrorist. He recruited my friend's son, and I think they are building a bomb."

"That is some shit."

"Yep."

"What are you gonna do?"

"I am gonna find them and stop them," V-man said.

"You two look deep in thought," AC said, stepping behind the bar in front of them.

"AC, I have lived in this town a long time. I have a bad feeling. I don't know where, and I don't know when, but someone is planning something big, and I have to stop it."

"I have the utmost faith in you, brother."

"I wish it were warranted in the case," V-man said.

"V-man, you know we always got your back. Just gotta tell us when and where," AC said in his gravelly voice.

"You have to be careful. Forrest is gunning for you, AC," Big Mike said, stepping into the conversation. "Don't make yourself stand out, or you are gonna lose this bar."

"Man, I don't give a shit about him. I ain't gonna leave my man hanging. Besides, he ain't gettin' this bar. They can't come in here, illegally seizing my assets."

"I wouldn't put anything past him."

"I don't want you getting in any trouble, AC. You have that boy to protect. You have to be a good example," V-man said, agreeing with Big Mike.

"What kind of example would I be if I let terrorists come up in here and blow shit up? Or left my friend out to dry? Like I said, you tell me when and where and I will be there," AC said.

"Therein lies the problem. I don't know when or where," he said, letting the frustration he felt come out in his voice.

A stretch of silence followed as V-man sipped his beer, Jay studied the counter, and AC and Big Mike studied V-man. There was a break-in at the Light Guard Armory on the east side on 8 Mile Road that had been reported on the news. They did not specify what was taken. V-man had watched the news intensively. He didn't believe in coincidence. He also knew C-4 explosives and weapons were stored there. V-man was restless and was walking around inside and outside the bar, briefly talking on his cell phone and sending out text messages. When he was like this, everyone left him alone. He would also go back in the kitchen with Jerome, teaching him old Italian recipes that were handed down from many generations. It was somewhat like therapy for him, and Jerome was a quick study, dramatically improving. He had just walked back into the kitchen when company arrived. Outside, six members of the Detroit Street Riders MC arrived. The DSR was one of the toughest biker clubs in the city. They were over 100 strong and were to be respected. They didn't necessarily fuck with anybody, but no one, and I mean no one fucked with these guys. As they dismounted, one guy who looked to be in charge, said a few words and two of the guys stayed with the bikes while four headed to the door. The in-charge guy said something else, and two of the guys stayed by the door while the leader and another guy came in. Big Mike and AC slowly slid off the bar stools. The two that entered clearly were the guys in charge. The leader, had "President" embroidered on one side of his vest and "Jethro" on the other side. He was an enormous man about six feet, six inches, with a proportioned build and at least 275 pounds. He had a striking resemblance to the TV Beverly Hillbillies actor, but there was no comedy with this man. The other guy had "Sergeant at Arms" on one side of his vest, and "MD" on the other. It stood for Mad Dog. He did resemble a huge six feet, two inch, 300-pound pit bull. He was a very scary guy who looked as though if he went off, you may slow him down with an elephant tranquilizer gun—if you were lucky. They walked in slowly, came toward to Big Mike and AC, and stopped a comfortable distance away. There the four stood, over a half ton of brute fucking ass-kickers for what seemed like a long time but was actually only seconds. They nodded ever so lightly, which was returned by the hosts. The DSR knew of the Corner Bar and paid it its deserved respect. Would be the same way had you came to the DSR Clubhouse. The president looked around and in a very serious tone asked, "Is he here?" And as if on cue, V-man walked out of the kitchen and looking at the two bikers, hesitated a moment, and said "You took

123

your fucking time getting here!" With that he headed over to the far corner of the bar, motioning for them to follow. The president glanced at the group, shook his head side to side, and followed, with MD loyally by his side. V-man was the only guy in the city to get away with a remark like that. He and Jethro went way back. They had ridden together for many years, and had backed each other's play on many occasions. And although V-man never joined the DSR, he was always welcome and had attended all their annual open houses, and was instrumental in negotiating their purchase of the clubhouse from the city, working through all the property violations. They also had the largest one-day fundraiser for the Michigan Vietnam Memorial being built in Lansing, the state capitol. That was the fundraiser that put the project over the top. Over 3,000 bikers attended and had the cooperation of all the local police and sheriffs' departments as well as the Michigan State Police. They blocked off entire streets and interstates as the huge caravan rode out to an amusement park that was donated for them exclusively for the entire day. And of course, V-man and Jethro were the leaders of the pack! Quite a sight and sound seeing and hearing 3,000 bikers! They were tight. Jethro's wife, a wild Georgia chick, known as "Big Angel," who was as tough as anyone in that club with a short temper to match, was like a wildcat released from a cage when she was pissed. She considered V-man as family. Her younger brother, Kenny, AKA "K-Boy" who rode with the club, had a liver problem years ago. It had progressed, and the only solution was a new liver. He was on the list for a transplant but was told that was a very long shot as the list was very slow process, which some people don't survive. It was a sad situation, and his sister and Jethro had taken him in to care for him with very little hope. Then, one night at 2:00 in the morning, they got the unexpected call to go immediately to Henry Ford Hospital; a donor had been found. Upon arrival, they whisked KBoy into surgery. After the room had cleared, looking around, she saw V-man sitting over in the corner.

"What fuck are you doing here?" And she immediately knew what had happened. She walked over to him, tears in her eyes, and gave him the biggest hug. V-man had glanced over at Jethro, and again, the big man of few words, gave him an up-and-down nod of his head, and V-man swore he saw a little mist in his eyes. V-man was a fixer, a doer. To him there was never a problem, just a situation, which always has a solution. Sometimes very difficult, but never impossible. He cherished his friendships, and there wasn't anything he wouldn't do for his friends.

V-man and Jethro sat at the table. V-man was describing something and looking intently at the president. The conversation lasted fifteen minutes, and the two guests got up and left. They again nodded to their hosts on the way out. Like a well-disciplined group, they started their motorcycles and rode off in unison, leaving that wonderful motorcycle sound in the air.

Chapter Fourteen

ANNA'S FINGERS REACHED FOR THE HANDGUN SHE
had stashed in the car in anticipation of another close-range fight. Now,
however, she wished her high-powered rifle was within closer reach. Her
fingers played along the cool, rough grip of the pistol. Not wanting to
betray her minimal advantage, she kept it hidden beside her thigh.

"Get out of the car. Hands up," came the shouts from her assailants
in thick, almost unintelligible accents.

Her fingers found the latch without taking her eyes off the barricade
of cars and angry men around her. A quick glance in the rearview mirror
showed the innocent people in cars running in the opposite direction.
But Rahim was still nowhere in sight. Some of those pedestrians were
probably calling the cops. If the cops came, it would all be over. She
would be taken to the station for questioning and lose the minimal trail
she may still have on Rahim.

The men in front of her crept closer as the hostility in their voice
ratcheted up. Anna sized up the challenge in front of her. The third
and fourth cars that had been pursuing her rumbled to screeching,
painful stops alongside the others. Two more guys got out of each new
car, making it six newly issued AK 47s to one SIG Sauer with a seven-
teen-round capacity. She didn't love those odds but with two additional

magazines, she could inflict serious damage if she could create a tactical advantage and isolate members of the group. A strange calm settled over her body, similar to the feeling she got when she hunted. Only this time, she wasn't hunting deer. Her breath became slow and rhythmic as her eyes focused on the targets in front of her. Her job was to survive, and she intended to do just that. Her DNA kicked in.

Her foot kicked open the car. With one smooth movement, her body rolled to the hard pavement, and she came up on one knee, steadied the pistol, and fired. The glass of her car window shattered as the bullet raced through. The man's head farthest to the left jerked backward before he crumpled to the pavement.

She knew that she would have to deal with the aftermath of her emotional trauma over killing a person when this was all over, but for now, her instincts were on autopilot. She ducked beneath the door as a barrage of bullets slammed the other side of her thin barricade. She scrambled back into the car and threw herself into the back seat. The gunfire didn't let up for a full minute. With her head ducked beneath the seat, out of view, she could only imagine how close the terrorists were getting. The sound of her breath came loudly in her ears. She closed her eyes and brought herself back to the familiar comfort of hunting in the woods, willing her heart rate to slow down. With the renewed peace, she heard a heavy foot crunching on the glass outside the front driver-side door that had been knocked out when she made her first shot. Twisting uncomfortably on the cramped floor of the back seat, she leveled her gun on the shoulder visible through the window.

She pulled the trigger. The man cursed and fell back, incapacitated but not dead.

Vito Anthony

"You have been causing a lot of trouble, little girl! I don't know why the men of this country let their women run free. It only causes them problems," a voice called toward the front of the car.

Anna found herself laughing at the remark. "Only small, insecure little men feel threatened by strong women. In this country, men have the balls to handle a girl like me!"

"Allah will bring retribution to you all! Have no doubt about that!" said the same voice.

"If you are so brave, little girl, then why don't you come out and face us?" Another voice said, closer to the car this time. From the sound, he was quickly approaching the rear passenger side door.

"I am tough, not stupid. Unlike you!" she shouted as she kicked open the car door, slamming it into the man standing close enough. He grunted and pulled his gun up to aim, but Anna was quicker. Her finger squeezed against the resistance, and the shot rang loud through the small space of the car.

Without thought or hesitation, she moved the weapon in the direction of the other man's voice, closer to the front of the car. She fired before taking careful aim and only managed to graze his shoulder. He lifted his weapon and pulled the trigger simultaneously with Anna. This was Anna's second chance, so she hit her mark dead on.

Searing pain blossomed in her left arm. She sucked in a sharp breath, trying to regain her level head, but the pain interfered with her concentration. She had taken out four men. That left three more. Looking up from the gash in her arm, she saw that one man stood leveling his gun at her on the opposite side of the car. The other was directly in front of her. Her head swiveled frantically trying to locate the third, but before she could, her head jerked back. Thick fingers were wrapped around her hair, and a dark face, twisted in anger, looked at her from behind. Her knees were at an odd angle so that she could see all of him, but she did notice the awful yellowed teeth showing through his nasty grin.

"We are going to have some fun with you," the man said. The slimy quality of his voice when he said "fun" made Anna's stomach turn.

"Drop your gun, or I will put a bullet between your eyes," said the man standing opposite her.

She did a quick calculation of her chances against three armed men before releasing her grip on the gun.

"We have her." One of the men picked up the walkie-talkie that had been clipped to his belt and spoke through it. The only sound she heard coming from the other end was crackling. Using her hair as a handle, the man pulled her away from her car and out into the open. He dragged her closer to the barricade of cars. The whole shootout couldn't have taken longer than a minute or two.

Behind her, she heard the sounds of more car engines. She craned her neck to see more beat-up old cars peeling into the open lanes of the highway. When they came to a stop, more terrorists piled out. She felt sick all over again. Even if she could have fought her way through three men, she couldn't fight her way through the small army lining up behind her. That was when she saw Rahim again. His familiar black car was parked off to the side, and he stepped out beside it.

He yelled across the open space in a language that Anna couldn't understand. The man at her side shouted back, gesturing toward Anna. They both sounded hostile and angry but were clearly on the same side. The conversation continued for a moment before the man who held her captive started pulling at her again, shoving her in the direction of his car.

The man pulled open the car door. Behind her, she heard the sound of car and truck engines again. She assumed the rest of the terrorists were on the move to carry out their plot. Her mind raced wildly as she tried to think of a way out of the awful, nightmarish fate that awaited her as a captive of these terrorists, but she couldn't think of anything reasonable. Then it occurred to her that she would probably be better off dead than as a hostage. With that thought in mind, she threw her head back with as much force as possible. The back of her skull made contact with the face of the man behind her.

"Hey!" he shouted in surprise. His grip didn't loosen, so she let her body weight drop, bringing his hand with it. While he was off balance, she swung her leg around behind her and swept his feet out from under him. He fell backward, bringing Anna with him. He lunged forward on hands and knees, grabbing her around her waist and hoisting her into the air.

A shot rang out. Anna squeezed her eyes shut. For a moment, she thought for sure this was the end. She wished that she had gotten to say goodbye to her brothers and father. But no new pain came. She slowly opened her eyes to a scene of chaos. The man behind her lay on the ground with a pool of blood forming around him. In front of her, the terrorists had turned their backs on her. Guns fired in the opposite direction. In front of them, three semi-trucks had pulled to a stop in a jagged horizontal line. Each truck depicted a familiar company logo well known in the thumb area of Michigan. One depicted a smiling young blonde girl holding a glass of milk, advertising a dairy farm neighboring Anna's own. It had been shot in the initial fray, and white liquid poured from the various holes in the tank of the truck.

Anna stood stunned for longer than was safe as she looked around, trying to make sense of what she watched. The report of gunfire, shouts, and frantic running men made her feel like she had been transported to a war zone. Using the trucks as barricades, a small militia of men took aim on the terrorists. The older man in the group was calling out directions. They had taken the terrorists by surprise. They were deer hunters, with very accurate high-powered rifles with scopes zeroing in on their targets. And one by one, the terrorists would meet their destiny and lay dead on the pavement.

She squinted as she hid behind the door of her car, trying to see who had come to her rescue. She knew that dairy company. Buddy's father was a truck driver for them. Realization dawned on her, and she felt stupid for taking so long to make the connection. But if Buddy had reached out over the CB radio, then her father and brothers knew where she was, and most likely, they were there, too.

The thought sent a cold chill down her back. If anything happened to them, it would be her fault. She couldn't let that happen. Anna looked around frantically for a gun, determined to do her part in the fight she had started. She debated trying to get her rifle out of the trunk, but worried it would put her in a vulnerable line of sight. Her gaze landed on the man lying dead on the ground at her feet. A gun was strapped to his back, pinned down by the weight of his body. She glanced around, making sure no one had noticed that her guard was no longer present, before bending to pick up the gun. The man's lifeless body must have weighed close to two hundred pounds, and the gun was wedged behind him with a strap across his chest. With all her strength, she tried pushing him over, her boots slipping through the blood that covered him. Finally, she managed to roll him onto his side and pull the gun free. Her weapons training at the academy had covered a lot of guns, but for the most part, she had only shot the less-common guns a handful of times. That included the AKs. Inexperience aside, it would be stupid to open fire and alert the terrorists to her presence without any cover.

Alongside the highway, a stretch of wild forest loomed just beyond the small shoulder of asphalt. It would provide the perfect cover to make it to the other side of the trucks where her family must be. Anna slung the gun over her back and crouched down behind the car that had almost become her tomb. She wove in and out of the parked and broken cars, recovered her service weapon, and found herself safely within the cover of trees and underbrush. It wasn't easy to walk through, but deer hunting gave her a pretty good foundation in traversing over grown foliage. The sound of the gunfire remained relatively constant. Here and there she heard stray shouts rise above the endless blasts of rapid fire. As she walked up the forest's edge parallel to the highway, the threat was beside her. She kept her eyes trained on the enemy, so she wouldn't be taken by surprise.

"Anna!" her father called. She startled at the sound of his voice so close by. When she looked up, she realized she had made it to the other side of the eighteen-wheeler. Oleksander looked at her from behind the truck. A few feet separated them. He somehow managed to look both tired and exhilarated at the same time. Sweat dripped down from his forehead, and he held a rifle in his hand, aimed at the terrorists across from the makeshift barricade. Further down, Ivan, Pavlo, Bobby, and Jimmy concentrated on the battle in front of them. None of them had any formal training in combat, and the tension of the situation showed on their face, but they managed to get the job done. They had never shot at anything that could shoot back, and although Anna had extensive training, she hadn't been in a real combat situation, either. Despite their inexperience, pride swelled in Anna's chest. They had all pulled through, doing their part without question. The natural tendency of deer hunters was to stay cool under fire. They had eliminated the terrorists very methodically.

She waited for the right moment before running to join her father.

"Dad! What are you doing here?" she asked when she was safely behind the truck.

"I am not letting my baby girl go off to save the world without some backup," he said.

"I am so sorry I dragged everyone into this," she said motioning toward her brothers and their friends.

"My little *Sol-nyshka moyo,* I have never been prouder of you. You saw a threat, and you didn't hesitate to fight for what was good and right. I raised you well. I just wish you had trusted your brothers and me to help you. Perhaps we could have done more good, sooner."

"I know, Father," she said.

He wrapped his free arm briefly around her before peeking around the truck again.

In the distance, barely audible over the gunfire, the wail of sirens announced the approach of the police. The sirens reminded her of what else was at stake. She looked from her family to the terrorists.

"I see your mind working," Olek said.

"I worry this is a distraction. I am sure the terrorists' plan wasn't intended to culminate in a highway shootout."

"You are probably right. But what then is it?"

Anna looked around the side of the truck again. "The leader of the group seems to be the man I have been trailing since he came into the country. It is possible that this cell already existed, and he was coming to finalize the plan, or he could have recruited these men since he got here. Either way, I think the key to the plot lies with him."

Olek studied his daughter, "What do you propose we do?"

Anna shrugged. "Stop him."

Olek laughed in his full-throated, gravelly way that instantly transported Anna to her childhood every time she heard it. He rubbed his hand on the top of her head. "Good plan. Don't run off by yourself again."

"I will try not to. I am going to walk the line of the trucks to see if I can find him,"

"Anna?" Olek said in the worried tone he always used when he felt like his baby girl was doing something too dangerous.

"Dad, you have to let me try to find him. I am the only one who knows what he looks like."

"I love you, Anna."

"I love you too, Dad." She gave him a kiss on the cheek as he turned his attention back to the fight.

Anna ran along the track, stopping at every opening to peer out. At the end of the line, she saw him. Rahim and a younger guy ducked low as they ran through the spray of bullets staying mostly behind the cars. The boy carried a blue book bag protectively in his arms rather than slung across his back. Anna took aim, but Rahim ducked behind a car before she had positioned herself for the shot. Rahim's now-familiar red car was clustered with a bunch of other cars that the terrorists had arrived in. He and his companion climbed inside. No one else seemed to notice them, or if they did, they didn't think it was important enough to stop them.

As they sped away, tearing across the small swath of grass that partitioned the east- and west-bound sides, to join the almost nonexistent traffic, Anna let out a frustrated sigh. Her head turned, looking for a way to follow. Then her eyes landed on Ivan's truck. Without thinking, she climbed into the driver's side. In the haste of the fight, he had left his keys in the ignition and a soft dinging sound resonated through the truck. She threw her newly acquired gun into the passenger seat and slammed the door closed. She threw the car into gear and took off after Rahim, who was headed back toward Detroit.

CHAPTER FIFTEEN

V-MAN HELD HIS HEAD IN HIS HANDS WHILE HIS elbows rested on the worn-out wood of the bar top. Jay sat beside him in the same place he had been the day before, as if he too was developing an assigned seat at the corner bar. AC poured coffee; Big Mike leaned up against the counter, talking to another patron who sat a few stools down, while Brenda wiped down tables in the main dining room. The TV blared the news of some sort of accident that turned into a shootout on interstate 94. It had pulled a large portion of the state and federal police force that had originally been called to the area for the expected protests at the trial away to the mess on the highway as the police chased those involved and investigated the scene. Something about the coverage perked V-man's attention. The media wasn't making any pronouncements about who was involved or what any of it meant, but V-man had a feeling it was all connected.

"I can't fucking find these guys! If they went underground, then we are out of time," V-man said, slamming his hand on the counter.

"Hey, mind the bar," Big Mike said, leaving his conversation with the other customer. "I will make you pigs in a blanket. No one can ever think on an empty stomach." He stepped out from behind the counter to go into the back.

V-man had no interest in eating. He had spent the prior evening, grilling the salesmen at the garden store. They admitted to remembering a couple of Middle Eastern men in the store, but dismissed it as normal business, saying they didn't discriminate based on race. They refused any attempts at trying to find out more detailed information about the type of car, the conversations they had, or what specifically they had purchased. V-man left frustrated and out of leads.

"I got something for ya," AC said, drawing V-man's attention. "Reached out to my man down on the East Side after we talked last night."

V-man turned to look directly at AC, who was slowly refilling the coffee filter with fresh grounds. "What'd you find?"

"Buddy of mine said some Middle Eastern mother fucker was down there day before last, talking to some of the younger guys, trying to convince them to join up with him. They ran him out of town pretty fast once they caught wind of his intentions."

"What did he say to them?" V-man asked. Big Mike resurfaced from the kitchen carrying a steaming plate of pigs in a blanket, which he put in front of V-man. He made a face and pushed the plate away in Mike's direction.

"You don't want them?"

"It is barely breakfast time," V-man said, shaking his head.

"Never stopped me," Big Mike said, picking up a hot dog wrapped in dough and popping it into his mouth while V-man shook his head again.

AC waited for Big Mike and V-man to be done with their conversation before he continued. "Nothing that would help you. He tried to convince them their life was shit and their country had turned their backs on them, and the only way to get anywhere was to join him."

"Did he tell them any details about his plan?"

"Nah, everything was vague," AC said.

"Damn it!"

"You so sure they have a plan?"

"Yes."

"How are we gonna find them then?" AC asked.

V-man smiled at his friend's support, although it didn't surprise him. When one of them had a problem, all of them had a problem. The only issue was that V-man didn't have an answer for him. The conversation faded into nothing as everyone pondered the circumstances. AC and Big Mike kept busy with cleaning, serving, and cooking for the guests that straggled in and out.

The door banged open with more force than was necessary. V-man looked up, ready to yell at whoever hadn't been raised to open doors properly. The group of four guys standing in the doorway wore all black from head to toe, including black bandanas wrapped around their faces, obscuring their features and making them impossible to identify. They wore heavy black combat books and some wore round red symbols on their jackets.

"Hey," the one in the front called rudely to Brenda. "Where's the bathroom?"

"Sorry, bathroom is for customers."

"Customers? You don't have any customers," he called as his friends laughed. From the sound of his voice, V-man guessed he was in his early twenties.

Brenda glared. "I suggest you find another restroom."

"We need to use your bathroom. No one else is in here. Just let us use it," the man said. "How are you gonna stop us?"

Brenda opened her mouth to speak, but before she could get any words out, V-man out of nowhere positioned himself between her and the gang of what he assumed were violent protesters.

"I am going to stop you," V-man said, clearly enunciating each word.

"Oh yeah, what about the rest of us?" He chuckled. The laugh died on his lips as AC and Big Mike stepped up behind V-man, crossing their arms over their chests. The men exchanged glances before exiting the bar. The leader however looked directly back at V-man. V-man was also watching him and many small groups just like his that were moving in the direction of downtown.

V-man made his way back to his seat with a growing tension of the pressure of the situation reaching down to his bones. Sitting still became an impossible task. He stood and walked the length of the bar. He stopped in front of the TV, which had been playing news coverage of the underwear bomber's trial and accompanying protests on a constantly repeating loop. Now, a pretty young brunette reporter stood on the steps of the local courthouse that was only a few blocks from the corner bar. Behind her, men dressed in suits stood in front of the courthouse. In front of her, a makeshift police barricade had been set up to corral the protesters. She was talking about the gathered people in front of her when the camera slowly panned to get a shot of the crowd.

The scene was chaos. Signs held high above people's heads displayed a wide variety of sentiments. V-man didn't mind the protests. He knew a lot of people on the right felt they were liberal snowflakes and those on the left thought the other protesters were right-wing racists. V-man just thought it was a display of the freedoms he had fought for so many years ago. The camera stayed trained on the crowd. V-man was about to turn away when he saw something that drew all his awareness to a fine point. He took an unconscious step toward the TV, staring closely, making sure what he thought he saw had been real and not a trick of his imagination. When he saw it again, he knew.

"Hey V, you gonna hurt your eyes staring at the TV like that," Jay said, still cupping his coffee mug in both hands.

V-man didn't hear Jay. He turned on his heels and walked briskly from the bar without a word to his friends. He finally had something. Outside, the sun was a stark contrast from the dim, almost gloomy lighting of the bar. V-man slipped a pair of tactical sunglasses over his eyes and walked a half block to where he had parked his Yukon. He hopped into the driver's side, started the engine, and with barely a glance behind him, he pulled out into the road. A car behind him honked in annoyance.

Pulling his phone from his pocket, he dialed Luca's number. After the third ring, he heard Luca's voice on the other end.

"Hey, Dad,"

"Luca, I need you to stay home today," V-man said.

"What? Why? What's going on now?"

"I can't get into it, but don't go anywhere and don't leave your apartment. Call your siblings and tell them the same thing. It isn't safe in Detroit today."

"Is it ever?"

"Funny," V-man said dryly. "I am not kidding. I need you to promise me you will stay inside."

"Okay, okay, Dad. I hope this isn't another one of your crazy theories," Luca said.

"I wish it was," V-man said. "I will call you when I know more."

With that, he hung up the phone just in time to pull in front of his house. He ran into the house, keeping his keys in hand. Taking the stairs two at a time, he arrived in his office, which had once been one of the kid's bedrooms, filled with bunk beds and toys, but now held a desk, filing cabinets, and stacks of paperwork. V-man went straight for the closet. Up at the top, on the highest shelf, he pulled down a heavy, silver-and-black hard-shelled case. He dropped it on the floor with a heavy thud. His fingers searched for the key ring before locating the correct one that fit smoothly into the lock on the box in front of him. The lid clicked open to reveal a small arsenal of weapons. Although his children no longer lived with him, he still felt better with his guns locked safely away.

He hesitated, looking at the guns, trying to decide on the best one for the task ahead. He started with a small survival knife that he strapped to his thigh. After that, he pulled out his new Smith & Wesson M 2.0 compact 9mm. In a crowd this would be easy to handle and very accurate at close quarters. Michigan was a concealed-carry state, and V-man had a permit that he carried on him at all times. A full-size older Browning High Powered 9mm with two fourteen-round magazines were in the driver side door in the map slot. This went with V-man everywhere. That was an additional option he would access upon arriving at the scene. He loaded his pockets with a two more magazines. The S&W M20 slid into the shoulder holster that he strapped on and fit nicely underneath his jacket that he zipped up. He was confident, with the Hornady Critical Duty 9mm+P FlexLock 135 Grain ammo, he had what he needed to get the job done if it came to that.

When he was satisfied with his preparations, he locked away the rest of the guns and made his way downstairs and back to his car. Walking to his vehicle he looked at his NRA Life Member sticker on his rear window. Thankful for the Second Amendment.

The center of Detroit was a logistic nightmare. Four or five blocks from the courthouse, traffic had stopped dead. Honking horns and the screams of irate motorists filled the air. V-man pulled into an open spot that he wasn't sure was a legal parking spot, but with the police occupying the rally up ahead, he didn't think he had to worry too much about a ticket. He did not take the larger 9mm.

Once on the street, he had to push his way through pedestrians who had stopped in their tracks to marvel at the traffic or catch a glimpse of the turmoil up ahead. V-man had the urge to warn everyone away, to yell at them to take shelter in their homes and avoid the imminent danger that was about to go down, but he knew it would come off as crazy, and instead focused himself on trying to prevent the almost inevitable tragedy.

Chapter Sixteen

THE CLOSER V-MAN GOT TO THE COURTHOUSE, THE more crowded the sidewalk and streets became. He had underestimated the size of the demonstration. The police had set up barricades using traffic cones, police tape, and temporary metal fences. People still climbed over and under them, but it at least prevented the traffic from getting through. Officers stood around with hands on belts, watching the mix of people move almost like waves in an ocean. The weather remained unseasonably warm, and V-man felt trickles of sweat down his back underneath his T-shirt and leather jacket. In his pocket, he felt his cell phone vibrate, indicating an incoming call. He ignored it. The courthouse itself, a historic building with a beige cement façade, loomed large in front of him. The giant building occupied an entire city block and stood many stories tall. The building was stark and unadorned by any ornamentation. On the streets surrounding it were similar gray buildings. Inside was a different story. Although it had been years since V-man had stepped foot into the federal courthouse, he knew the original architects in the 1930s had made a point of creating cathedral ceilings, and ornate hand-carved railings throughout the lobby.

Now, however, the building swarmed with people. The demonstrators poured in from side streets, trying to cram into the small section of blocked-off road on West Lafayette Street. They spilled past the barricade onto the south side of the building onto Fort Street, carrying signs and waving flags. The police did their best to keep the two disagreeing groups separated, but the lines seemed to be breaking down. Chants sprang up, from one corner or another, and then were quickly picked up by the rest of the crowd, followed quickly by some counter chant on the other side.

V-man stood at the end of the street, watching the wall of people waving their brightly colored signs and shouting incoherently at no one in particular. He eyed the police officers. Their posture was tense, and he saw a few hands inching closer to side arms. V-man shook his head. If they only knew the real threat, no one would be concerned about a bunch of Americans yelling at each other.

V-man felt his chest tighten. He took a deep breath and stepped into the crowd. No one took notice of him. Everyone was too busy with their own interests to be bothered with a middle-aged man jostling through the crowd. Up ahead, he saw the reporter from earlier still in front of the camera. Now she was interviewing a young woman. The woman was waving her hands and talking enthusiastically, but he couldn't hear the reporter's question or the woman's answer. V-man's eyes scanned the people around him, trying to catch nuances in a wall of chaos. Faces faded together, creating a blur of motion and activity. A white man with a side arm cupped his hands around his mouth, shouting in the direction of another man who angrily waved a sign that read "America First." A black woman wearing a "Black Lives Matter" T-shirt waved a hand-written sign with the words, "Not all Muslims are terrorists." V-man dismissed them and pushed forward. His elbows jostled those around him roughly. He didn't have time to step lightly. In the process, he felt himself being pushed, sometimes accidentally and other times with a purposeful force.

Despite the roiling tension, it all seemed innocuous to V-man. Americans exercising their First Amendment right, whether he agreed or not, didn't bother him much. He wondered how these people would react if they knew the threat facing them at this very moment. Would they band together? He would like to think so, although some would call that overly optimistic.

From the corner of his eye, he caught sight of a wisp of blonde hair that alerted some memory in the back of his mind. It wasn't the person he had been looking for, but seeing the vaguely familiar face here felt like too much of a coincidence. This was the third time he had seen the young blonde woman in the general vicinity of Rahim. V-man had a tendency to remember every face he saw, and this young girl with her pretty features and clean-cut look was no exception. V-man stopped walking to study her. She didn't look like part of either rally. She didn't carry a sign and wasn't yelling, but beneath her jacket, he thought he saw an outline of a hand gun. Her eyes were set in a hardened stare as she looked around with tense purpose. She paused only briefly before continuing through the crowd.

What could have transpired to drag this young girl into a mess with a terrorist? V-man turned on his heels to follow her, keeping one eye trained on the blonde hair bobbing up and down through the crowd, while surveying with the other. The girl changed directions a few times and didn't seem to have any end goal in mind as she shifted through the swarm of people. The longer he followed, the more frantic she seemed to become. Eventually, V-man stopped trailing so far behind and moved to catch up.

He came up beside her and gently touched her elbow. She nearly jumped out of her skin before quickly moving into a defensive stance. V-man wasn't classically trained in martial arts, but he knew a fighter when he saw one.

"What?" she said. Her eyes darted around to the people surrounding them. V-man had already taken stock of their environment. Directly behind him, there was a small circle of college-age kids holding their smart phones above their heads, recording the rally around them. Behind the girl, a man around V-man's age was singing a protest song from the '70s that didn't seem to fit the occasion, but probably meant something to the guy singing. On the sides, the crush of relentless people pushed against them.

"I have seen you before," V-man said.

The girl's face twisted in a mixture of disgust and confusion, "Uh huh, sure," she said before turning to go.

"What brings you here?" V-man said.

"I am very busy. I don't have time to talk."

"Neither do I," he said. "I think we might be here for similar reasons. The last time I saw you was at the local Arabic cultural center. You were driving a green Cherokee."

This gave the girl pause. "How did you see me?"

"You were across from me at an intersection," V-man said. "I didn't think anything of it, but then I saw you again outside of my friend's place."

She squinted her eyes at him, trying to figure out what his angle was.

"You want to know what those two places and this place all have in common?" he asked.

"Okay," she said skeptically.

"One man. His name is Rahim. You know him?" V-man said. The girl's face flashed with surprised recognition before she settled back into a neutral expression, not betraying any inner thoughts she might have in relation to Rahim's name.

"I have heard of him."

"How would a girl like you get mixed up with a guy like Rahim?"

"How would a man like you get mixed up with a guy like Rahim?" she asked, lifting her eyebrows.

V-man looked intently at her. Despite the dire situation, he found he liked the girl's fiery personality. "All right. From the moment I met Rahim, I recognized that something was off with him. I have been working hard to find out. I think he is up to something very dangerous. If you have somehow been brought into his plot, you have to know that whatever he has been telling you is all lies."

She now assessed V-man. "She shook her head. "I know he is up to something very dangerous. That is why I am here. I am Border Patrol and have been tracking him.

"How did you know he was here?" Anna asked.

"I saw him walking through the crowd when the news camera panned over the rally. I am certain they are planning on setting off an explosive to create chaos and kill as many Americans as they can.

She nodded. "He had also planned to have a lot more backup, but my friends and I put a stop to that. He is desperate and alone now. We have to find him quickly."

"I wouldn't be surprised if he has more guys than the ones you ran into. Typically, these guys are either lone wolf types, or they are backed by the larger terror group. Don't let your guard down, thinking we only have one enemy. We might very well be surrounded."

Anna looked worried.

"That gun you are carrying needs to be your last resort. Any one of them could be packing explosives, and gunfire in such tight quarters would be disastrous."

"Okay," she said quietly. The furrow in her brow deepened. "But how do we find him?"

"This was a well-planned out attack. He obviously has no hope of getting inside, so where would a bomb in this crowd be the most effective?" V-man said almost more to himself.

"That depends on his goal," Anna said thoughtfully. "If he wants to kill the most innocent people, then that would be in the center of the rally. If he wants to damage the building in the hopes of retrieving the 'underwear bomber,' that would be close to the building."

V-man nodded, impressed with her reasoning. He looked around at the gathered people, lost in thought for a moment.

"If he really had planned to have backup, then he wouldn't need to kill people with the bomb," V-man said.

"Then I think we should assume he planned on using the bomb for the building."

"Agreed. It is the safest assumption at this point." He cased the crowd and the building with a new perspective. "The police presence is heaviest at the intersections. He would move into the middle. That would also be the best place for maximum damage to the building. If any backup does make it here, they will most likely try to infiltrate the crowd. Be prepared for them to be among innocent bystanders. I will start at the southwest corner. You start at the northwest corner."

Anna nodded. V-man could tell she was nervous, but he admired her strength to continue. Her expression was one of grim determination. She probably felt the same responsibility he did. They seemed to be the only two people with the ability to prevent a massive terror plot.

V-man nodded toward Anna, silently showing his support. He turned away and made his way to the corner of the building.

"What the hell was that?" Jay asked watching V-man retreat from the bar.

"Who knows with him?" AC said, shrugging.

"Where do you think he is going?"

"Man, your guess is as good as mine."

Jay looked around the mostly empty bar. It was off-peak hours for the three main meals of the day. The breakfast crowd had recently dispersed, and the lunch crowd hadn't yet arrived. A few locals sat at the bar, nursing beers despite the early hours. Big Mike pushed through the doors from the back.

"Where did V-man go?" he asked.

"I was just asking the same thing," Jay said. He had come back to Detroit to keep an eye on V-man and here he was sitting alone at a bar, losing him after only a few hours back in the city. "I have a bad feeling."

Big Mike, AC, and Jay all sat in the relative silence of the mostly empty bar, contemplating where their friend might be.

"Hey guys."

They all turned to see Homer walking into the bar with his typical carefree grin across his face.

"Homer," Big Mike said. "How's it going?"

"Pretty good."

"You got a delivery or something?" AC asked.

"Nah, it's my day off. Just came in to hang out with Big Mike."

"That's my boy," Big Mike said, proudly wrapping his large arm around his shoulder.

"Do you think he might be right? About the terror plot?" Jay asked, interrupting the tender moment.

"The better question is, do you think he might need help?" AC asked.

"What's going on?" Homer asked, but everyone ignored him.

Jay pulled his cell phone out of his pocket and dialed V-man's number. After the fourth or fifth ring, Jay hung up before he got to voicemail. If only he knew who had written the letter, he might have a better sense of what kind of danger V-man was walking blindly into. On a hunch, he looked up the phone number belonging to the house that he and V-man had visited, looking for Valenzuela that went to voicemail. Instead of a person, it was a mechanical, female voice, asking him to leave a message. The kind of greetings that come standard on phones.

"Valenzuela, if this is you, it's Jay. Give me a call. It's about V-man," Jay said into the phone before hanging up. He didn't want to say more in case it wasn't Valenzuela phone.

Behind him, he heard shouts coming from the nonstop coverage of the rally happening downtown. In DC, people seemed to start up rallies and protests on their lunch breaks. It wasn't anything unusual, and Jay didn't pay much attention. This one dominated the news cycle in Detroit, and because of its size and reason, the national attention had turned to it. The numbers were estimated to be in the thousands. Jay remembered the "underwear bomber." Despite the ridiculous name given to him by the media, it had been a chilling example of the lengths terrorists would go to in the name of their unhinged ideas. Jay was glad the trial had finally come and hoped justice was served. He had always considered himself a moderate, politically, but he had seen one too many deaths at the hands of radicals to want anything other than the death penalty for this sicko.

He turned to watch the rallies as the newscaster discussed the time line for the trial. Jay watched as people shouted and police tried to maintain some semblance of control. When he saw V-man come on screen, he sighed and shook his head.

"What the hell is he up to?" he asked no one in particular. V-man stood in the thick of the crowd. It looked like he was talking to a young blonde woman.

"You know V-man, he's always gotta be in the mix somehow," AC said, watching the TV now, too. The camera had since panned away from V-man's location. Nothing looked unusual about the rally. It was, of course, larger than most. The mass of people snaked through the streets of Detroit, stopping traffic. From what Jay could tell during the brief shots provided by the news, no one had gotten violent yet. What could have sent V-man racing out of the bar to join the rally? That wasn't like him at all.

"Well, I guess it's time to go," Big Mike said, putting on a light jacket.

"Brenda, keep an eye on things here," AC said.

Jay stood while AC stepped out from behind the bar. All three rushed toward the door with Homer trailing behind.

"Jerome?" AC's voice carried through the bar and was loud enough to be heard in the back. "We gotta go. Come on."

Jay pulled out the keys to his rental car. "My car is parked right over there," he said pointing.

"Man, I think I should drive. I know this city," AC said, eyeing the car and Jay in turn.

Jay held onto the keys. "You aren't part of my rental agreement."

AC laughed. "Shit man, ain't no one reads rental agreements. Give me the damn keys." AC didn't own a car. He relied mostly on public transportation to get to the few places he needed to be.

Jay raised his eyebrows. "When was the last time you drove?"

"The '80s."

"I really think I should drive."

"We don't have time for this," Big Mike interjected.

"We can take my truck," Homer said. "It's right here." He pointed to the pick-up truck double- parked in front of the bar. Big Mike smiled approvingly while Jay and AC both shared a look before climbing into the bed of the truck as Jerome stepped out of the bar, looking around with confusion.

"Get in, boy," AC said. "We gotta provide V-man with some back up."

Jerome nodded before realizing the only available spot was beside Homer in the cab of the truck. Big Mike and AC, the monsters of the midway, took up the majority of the bed with their hulking mass. Jerome shot Homer a look that conveyed his disdain before climbing in.

"Hey," he said.

"Hey," Homer said with an equal chip to his voice.

In the back, AC, Jay and Big Mike settled in as much as possible for the ride to the courthouse, trying to keep their eyes sharp for any trouble. AC felt a tap on his shoulder and looked to Big Mike, who motioned his attention toward the rear window of the cab, where a large confederate flag sticker clung to the glass. AC and Big Mike exchanged a smile. Homer was proud of it. It was his heritage.

The ride to the courthouse was stop and go at best. Eventually the traffic stopped dead as people and abandoned vehicles clogged the roads. Homer put the truck in park and abandoned it for the time being to make the rest of the trek on foot.

They pushed through the crowd and wove through the street that had become a glorified parking lot. Sounds of shouting reached them well before they laid eyes on the courthouse. When the building finally came into view, they could not have been prepared for what they saw.

CHAPTER SEVENTEEN

THE CROWD SEEMED TO BE GETTING DENSER BY
the minute as V-man tried to comb through it, while standing beside
the barricade keeping the rally from encroaching on the building. V-man
was known for his eagle eyes, but even he had a hard time keeping
track of every movement going on around him. People moved around
waving hands, shaking fists, and holding signs. At any given moment,
his peripheral vision was blocked by a poster or flag or body in the way.
The poor line of sight and imminent threat of unseen attack was vaguely
reminiscent of his time in 'Nam. How did his own city streets become
a battle zone?

To his left opposite the building, the shouting took on an angrier
tone. He turned just in time to deflect a fist coming toward the side of
his head. He managed to duck down and avoid another blow. In doing
so, he stumbled back into innocent people who turned startled eyes on
the sudden outburst of violence. V-man looked up to find a grinning
Rahim standing next to him. His jacket was tightly fit. It didn't look like
it could conceal a bomb. V-man was both relieved and worried about
this revelation. If Rahim didn't have it, then where was it?

"Not so tough now?" he said, to which V-man slammed his foot
into his chest, wiping the grin off his smug face. Rahim fell backward,

landing in the crowd. The stranger who caught him shoved him back in the direction of V-man. Rahim, in turn, used his forward momentum to slam into V-man. When he realized the element of surprise had been used up, and V-man wouldn't be such an easy target to take down, he took off through the crowd. V-man took off after him, jostling through the crowd. He skidded to a stop when a large Middle Eastern–looking man stepped out in front of him. He lifted his navy blue duster jacket to reveal an AK47 hiding underneath.

Time slowed to a standstill as V-man debated his next move. He couldn't let the terrorist loose on the crowd packing serious weaponry, but he also couldn't let the greater threat get away. Clearly, the terrorist had plans and backup plans. If Rahim couldn't detonate the bomb, then they would probably just open fire. One way or another, they were determined to kill as many Americans as possible. V-man clenched his first and threw the first punch. The guns and bombs had made the terrorists overly confident. They seemed to assume no one would try to stop them if they touted big firepower. They hadn't counted on V-man. He had faced down worse shit than this before.

The terrorist faltered from the punch. When he recovered, he reached for his gun. Before he managed to get it out and aim effectively, Anna stepped up beside him, swinging the butt end of her hand gun, smashing him in the face. V-man looked up at her and nodded.

Where is Rahim?" Anna said.

"Up ahead. Make sure this guy doesn't get up again," V-man said, taking off again. As he ran, he spared a parting glance in Anna's direction to see another terrorist approach. He had to trust that Anna could handle it. With the increased violence of the terrorists trying to stop Anna and V-man, the crowd around him was getting both restless and suspicious. They moved in huddled groups. Their shouts were angrier and less peaceful. Fearful bystanders mixed in with violent terrorists was a dangerous mix. The behavior of civilians in dangerous, combat-like situations was unpredictable at best.

Ahead, Rahim had stopped moving. Carefully, V-man approached until he had a direct line of sight through the crowd. Rahim stood in front of another, shorter man. His fingers fumbled hurriedly with some straps and bands coming off of the man's clothing in front of him. As he got closer, V-man's heart stopped in his chest. The boy standing opposite Rahim was all too familiar to V-man, wearing a heavy jacket, too heavy for the heat wave. The implication settled heavily across V-man shoulders and gave him a moment's pause. In that split second, Rahim finished his task and turned to see V-man. Without hesitation, he charged V-man. Behind him, Jasim turned and ran. V-man opened his mouth to shout at Jasim, but found himself in hand-to-hand combat with Rahim.

The man's skills were lacking. It quickly became clear that he had no formal training in martial arts or any other type of hand-to-hand combat techniques. But what he lacked in technique he made up for with a pure burning hate that radiated through his whole body. Every swing, every kick, was filled with the venom of a man who had already lost everything. There was nothing for Rahim after this moment in time. He had dedicated his life to this one singular pursuit. The threat that V-man and Anna represented was anathema to the very core of Rahim's soul if he even had a soul. Not one worth saving anymore, at least.

The V-man struggled to stay up against the constant flurry of punches that didn't let up even for a second. He managed to block most, but Rahim landed a few solid hits to V-man's body. V-man watched Rahim carefully during the melee. Finally, after a few minutes, he saw what he had been looking for. Signs of fatigue. Sweat dripped down his dark brown skin, and his punches started coming slower. V-man took his chance, swinging his leg out and knocking Rahim off balance. He stumbled. The crowd around them shouted in their direction and pushed at them whenever either of them got too close, but for the most part no one was ready to jump in yet. It wasn't unusual at protests like this one for fights to break out. People shouted, egging the fighters on. The police did what they could, but their presence was spread far too thin. There was a high likelihood that the protests would turn south, and it may or may not be V-man's fault. V-man recovered enough to throw a heavy fist into Rahim's jaw, completing the process of bringing Rahim to the ground.

V-man heard a gunshot, and a sinking dread made his veins run cold, worrying about Anna. At the sound of the first gunshot, the crowd seethed in panic. People started screaming and pushing, trying to get as far from the shot as they could. The acoustics of the city streets and tall buildings made the sound echo, making it impossible to determine exactly where the gunfire had come from. The police all pulled weapons and tried to direct the crowd from the shots fired, but even they were helpless in the fight against an unseen enemy. V-man almost lost hold of Rahim during the chaos as he tried to pull away.

The gunshot was only the first of many.

Anna felt the firm grip of a hand wrap around her forearm before it yanked her off balance. During her training, she had been at the top of her class in jujitsu, and she pursued it even outside of school, but she had only ever practiced it in safe, calm, preplanned melees. She realized quickly that her uncertainty was giving her adversary the upper hand.

The protesters around them had formed a circle. No one was sure why the two were fighting or who was on which side, so the trepidation prevailed, causing most of the spectators to either record the incident on their phones or simply yell into the void.

Her breath became choppy gasps as all her focus went toward avoiding the swings.

As her vision threatened to go black and flashing pinpoints filled her vision, a calm rage filled her, bringing with it crystal-clear awareness of the men around her. Underneath the hardened pretense of power were pathetic young men, terrified of their own hollow fragility in a changing world, desperate to hide their ineptitude with aggression. She didn't feel any fear. She wasn't some helpless damsel, needing saving. Her training kicked in. Another man came around behind her and wrapped his arms around her, pinning her arms to her sides. She lifted her leg and kicked into the first assailant's chest, flipping over the man who held her, twisting out of his arms. The man she kicked fell to the ground. The other man looked at her with surprise. The expression didn't last long because she did him the favor of wiping it off his face with the bottom of her boot. Blood sprayed in a wide arc from his nose. If she had to guess, she would say it was broken. Behind him, the other man stood up. He didn't look surprised. He looked angry.

She put a mocking frown on her face. "Poor guy," she said before landing a roundhouse kick into his chest.

"You bitch," he grunted as he stumbled into the crowd.

"So disrespectful of the person handing you your ass on a platter." The trash talk was outside of her normal repertoire, but she couldn't leave her anger unspoken.

He charged her. It was easy for her to fall into a jujitsu stance, throw him off balance and pin him to the ground. She knelt on his arms, preventing him from getting up. The entire fight probably only lasted a minute, but she was out of breath. She also hadn't planned for what to do once they were down. The hair on the back of her neck stood up a second before she heard the click of a pistol being readied behind her.

"Not so confident now?" His face was a mask of blood, but she could just barely see the crooked teeth forming a grin beneath his mustache. He said the words as if her confidence was an insult to his existence.

He wouldn't let her live. There was no point. She was more trouble than she was worth. He was going to pull that trigger. It was only a matter of when and what she could do between now and then.

"With the threat of real gun violence, the crowd backed up further. No one willing to be a hero. The man's grin grew wider, blood dripping from his lips to run through the gaps in his teeth.

"You always think you are so tough, but you are nothing."

This brief pause gave her the opportunity she was hoping for as she carefully reached her fingers around the arms of the man on the ground. He wasn't a big man. She guessed he weighed in around one-sixty at most. If she threw her weight in just the right way, her plan would work.

"Did you hear me?" the man shouted. He had lowered his gun slightly during his questioning.

Anna turned her head to look at him, this time all pretense of tears gone. "Fuck you!" As soon as the words left her lips, she threw her body to the side, rolling onto the hard ground and lifting the other man on top of her. The shot fired. She felt the man's body jerk violently and warm wet drip onto her shirt. Her gun slid smoothly from its position at her belt. She pulled the trigger. The man in front of her flew backward in a spray of blood that splattered the crowd. The screams started almost instantly, followed by a stampede as people pushed and shoved away from the gore that surrounded Anna.

With one fist wrapped around Rahim's jacket collar, the V-man's other fist coiled into a tight ball before landing solidly on Rahim's face. His head snapped back from the impact.

"Where is Jasim planting that bomb?" V-man asked.

Rahim spit out blood-tinged saliva but didn't respond. V-man threw him down to the ground, pinning his face against the rough pavement with a knee in his back.

"You aren't getting out of this," V-man said. Around him, people ran and screamed. The gunshots from Anna's direction had emboldened the protesters, who already had a natural proclivity toward violence, to begin acting out toward their counter protesters. In the midst of the running pedestrians and protesters who held their ground, small scuffles added to the chaos. V-man didn't worry about the scuffles among Americans. He worried about more terrorists unloading on the unarmed, unsuspecting crowd.

"Why would I tell you? I never planned to live through the day. I am a humble servant of Allah. You cannot touch me," Rahim said through gritted teeth.

"How about I keep you alive? You can rot in prison, a failure," V-man said. Another gunshot broke through the ruckus. A second later, an enormous force hit V-man's shoulder, followed by a searing pain. He had been lucky enough to make it through all of Vietnam without experiencing a single bullet wound, despite what a lot of people considered a reckless attitude. Now that he had the experience, it hurt like hell. His hand found the wound. Blood ran down, soaking his shirt and jacket. Beneath him, Rahim bucked and squirmed while V-man studied his wound, throwing V-man to the ground, sending new pain streaking down his arm.

Through the perspiration that dripped into his eyes, he saw a Muslim male walking toward him with big strides, a large gun held in his hands, preparing to take aim at V-man again. A chill ran down his spine when he realized he wasn't the only armed man making his way through the crowd. Guns fired off in the distance as the other terrorists revealed themselves and began intimidating the crowd. No explosion had gone off yet, and the armed men hadn't opened fire, which meant he still had some time.

V-man scrambled to his knees, gritting his teeth against the now-constant ache in his shoulder. He pulled his gun to take aim at the approaching man, but Rahim wrapped his hands around V-man's forearm and pulled him off balance. V-man didn't dare take the shot while struggling to keep the gun steady for fear he would hit an innocent. The two men wrestled on the ground for control of the gun while the other man approached to tip the balance in Rahim's favor.

V-man startled at the crack of a gunshot right behind him. The terrorist who had been approaching him from behind fell in a heap. V-man looked around before laying eyes on a Hispanic man sitting in a wheelchair. His legs had been amputated long ago. V-man remembered the detonation that had taken them and the bone-chilling panic that had accompanied it when they pulled Valenzuela from the foxhole. Valenzuela raised his hand to his forehead and saluted V-man before moving out of sight. A swell of enormous pride and gratitude threatened to choke him. After all these years, there was his Army buddy, friend, and brother getting his back again. It was then that V-man noticed Gomez and the guys from Valenzuela's neighborhood moving through the crowd taking directions from LaBamba.

With the second man bleeding out on the asphalt, V-man focused everything on Rahim. His arm felt weak, and he didn't know how long he would be able to hold onto the gun. The gunshots around him were getting more frequent. The terrorists were making their move to begin a systematic blood bath of anyone who got in their way. The sound of boots thundering on pavement, panicked screams, and gunfire created a cacophony in the narrow street in front of the courthouse. Protesters had finally taken the hint that something more than minor disagreements plagued the rally and ran in earnest for their lives. Despite trying to empty out of the street quickly, it was a slow process. The street became a bottleneck on both ends, and there was little space for the thousands of people to go.

All around him, he recognized the people fighting back against the terrorists. The cavalry had arrived. "He is trampling out the vintage where the grapes of wrath are stored" thought the V-man as he viewed good vs evil. His Faith was always with him .It had carried him thru the Hells of Vietnam and today would be no different.

AC, Jay, and Big Mike stood at the edge of what was left of the blockade. The wooden sawhorses and orange cones that had marked the road closure were broken and shattered across the ground. The officers they would have expected to be supervising the barricade had dwindled to two or three uniformed men who crouched behind cars and debris with guns drawn, skittishly awaiting whatever threat they had perceived. The press of people coming in the opposite direction and filing into the street and sidewalk crushed against them, making it hard to stand their ground. People pushed violently, trying to get out of the thin opening leading to the intersection of another cross street. Traffic hadn't been stopped here, but the cars could barely move while the crowd worked their way through.

The sound of gunfire ahead made AC look up sharply. The cops beside him shifted nervously, sharing an "Oh shit" look. They probably spent most of their career dealing with individual criminals, never facing multiple threats. AC spared a brief thought for Chief Williams and how he was fairing.

"You guys ready?" Jay said. He was infantry trained and immediately took the point. The tall basketball player could not bear the thought of V-man needing help and him not being there. AC and Big Mike were right there with him in the "unspoken bond"!

"Let's have some fun," Big Mike said. "Stay close, boys," he said to Jerome and Homer as they positioned the younger guys behind Jay and in front of the two big men.

Making their way closer to the building wasn't easy. A shared anxiety had overcome the peaceful protesters. The only people not trying to force themselves into any space available away from the courthouse were those trapped by the already slow-moving crowd, those in the midst of a fight, or the terrorists. It was easy to spot the terrorists. Not for the usual reasons of clothes or skin color, but because of their expressions of grim satisfaction and determined bravery, if it could be called bravery at all, which AC didn't. A lack of concern for life, including their own, wasn't bravery. It was the ultimate cowardice.

They wove through the people, fighting every step of the way. The five were like a combat unit, protecting each other on all fronts. They came upon the group that tried to get into the Bar. With their clubs and other weapons, they moved into the five from the side, eager to inflict some pain. Homer pulled Jerome out of the way of a swinging club that barely missed his head. They tangled with this group for what seemed like hours, but in a matter of minutes, the guys dressed in black were totally disarmed and disabled. Especially the leader—Jay made certain he got that message beating him to the ground with a barrage of punches knocking him unconscious. You don't fuck with 'Nam Brothers.

With shots being fired, the situation was getting very serious. This was much bigger that just a protest, and it was about to get worse. The larger portion of the guys in black just showed up. One hundred-plus as V-man spotted them coming through an alley between the old buildings. This was by design, as they had sent in small groups first to cause as much chaos as possible. These guys were organized and well equipped. Had he totally underestimated their numbers? They starting moving directly toward him and his small groups, which would be severely outnumbered.

His mind was racing. Would they prevent him from stopping the bombing that would kill so many? He would never forgive himself. He stood as if he was frozen and everything around him seem to go to slow motion. It seemed like time stood still. And then a sound that was faint began to get louder. A familiar sound. A welcoming unmistakable sound, as 100-plus bikers of the DSR rounded the corner roared into the area with people diving out of their way.

A sense of confidence and appreciation crept back into V-man. Jethro had mobilized the entire club, including the "Old Ladies." They came storming in and were there to do business. They dismounted their bikes, and the new guys and "Old Ladies' were in charge of securing them. Jethro, Mad Dog, and the entire club wasted no time and engaged the new large group that was busting windows and creating havoc and beating up on defenseless people. Their "party" was about to be over. The guys in black were no match for the hardened bikers who immediately began to eliminate them as a factor. "He has loosed the fateful lightning of His terrible swift sword" thought V-man.

V-man watched as Jethro and Mad Dog and the DSR were delivering a major dose of kickass as they totally dismantled the newly arrived group. Those protesters were learning what most people already knew. Nobody comes to their city and fucks with the DSR. Meanwhile, back at the parked DSR bikes, a situation was developing. There was a large, weirdly dressed women's group that wore outfits and hats that were all the different private parts of the female body. They were a smart-ass disrespectful group and were trashing the area and stomping on American flags as they headed toward the protest. As they were passing the parked DSR cycles, some of them were discarding coffee and beverages and splashed some of the bikes. When one of the new guys from DSR approached the group, one of the group, in a sarcastic tone, challenged the biker and said, "What are going to do, tough guy, hit a woman?" which drew laughter and other remarks from all those around her.

What see had failed to see was Big Angel and company,who had been watching intently,, like a group of lioness protecting the pride. In seconds, Big Angel was on her and with a "Fuck you, bitch" and smashed her fist to the side of her head, knocking her off her feet with bells ringing in her head. She had barely hit the ground, and the biker chick was dragging her by hair away from the bikes. That was the cue as the remainder of the "Old Ladies" tore into the group. They had names like "Dragon Lady" a Cambodian refugee who had escaped the Khmer Rouge, "Ink" who had more tattoos than anyone in the club who was an orphan and had raised herself on the streets of Detroit, "Cajun" a wild Creole chick from Louisiana, "Mamma Bear," a big strong mountain girl form Colorado, "Stiletto" who always wore all black and had the sharpest pointed boots, which she was making good use of. And dozens more of these tough real American women who had a message of their own to send. "Nobody, and I mean nobody, stomps on our flag and nobody fucks with the DSR!" They had scattered the entire group in less than fifteen minutes and grabbed all the American flags that were being disrespected.

In all the commotion, AC and Chief Williamson came face-to-face. AC held his gaze momentarily, and the Chief did the same. Whatever differences they had could wait. This was not the time for petty bullshit. "The V-man is here somewhere! He is convinced something big is going to happen. "He yelled over to the Chief.

The chief looked around. His eyebrows furrowed, and his eyes squinted as his mouth drew into a thin line. There were lots of factions here. A powder keg was lit, just waiting to explode. People milling about, trying to decide if they should risk the violence to continue protesting, squabbles between counter protesters, and a fist fight off to their right. "It looks like a protest gone bad to me."

"Worse than you think. Try looking closer. You see that fucker, skulkin' around over there?" AC pointed to someone he was sure was a terrorist. The man wore a baseball cap low over his eyes and studied the crowd without being part of it. His heavy jacket moved awkwardly, signifying it wasn't flush against his body. During the brief time they watched him, he reached his hand into his jacket twice. "Whose side do you think he is on?"

The chief studied the man in question for another moment. The confusion that had dominated his face was slowly replaced by a sinking suspicion and a vague flash of realization. "Who are they?"

"According to V-man, we think terrorists," AC said.

Chief gave him a concerned look.

"I don't know for sure, but they ain't Americans, and they ain't here to exercise their First Amendment rights. V-man thinks they have a bomb."

The chief thought for a quick moment. As much as the V-man sometimes drove him to the brink, he respected his reputation and his undying love for his country.

"We got to find him. He needs us.

The chief opened his mouth to say more, but AC had already turned his back and started walking away. They hadn't heard another gunshot, and the crowd had stopped running so frantically. The state of constant motion almost made it harder to make their way through. AC pushed his way into a clearing where people had gathered to watch something of interest. AC knew before he even saw his eyes confirmed that it was V-man. On the ground, V-man wrestled a Middle Eastern guy. He seemed to have the upper hand, but AC's instinct made him want to jump in and tip the balance further. Before he could make his way to the front of the circled-up people, a shot rang through the air.

AC looked up to see the gun pointed at V-man. He pulled people out of the way, not caring if they got hurt in the process. The distance between him and the other guy was closing too slowly. He wasn't going to make it in time to stop him from shooting again. Another shot rang out, this time behind him. The man flew backward. AC didn't bother looking behind him. He didn't care who had shot the terrorist, as long as the man behind him was on his side. In front of him, two more terrorists materialized out of the crowd.

Big Mike's thick fingers tapped AC's shoulder to get his attention. When AC's gaze tracked along Mike's pointed finger, he saw two more terrorists approaching from the opposite direction. They were outnumbered and outgunned.

"You take those two; I will take these. Take 'em by surprise, so they can't pull weapons," AC said.

He walked toward the two approaching terrorists, trying to adopt an air of worry, like the other protesters, but when he got with arm's reach, he sprang into action.

As the crowd began thinning again with the latest gunshots, V-man caught sight of AC working furiously as he threw his fist into the back of an unsuspecting terrorist who struggled to get his gun out. A spray of blood misted into the air as AC made contact with the back of the man's skull. AC landed another punch as the terrorist fell to the ground, making sure he didn't get back up again. As soon as he finished that guy, he turned on the next one.

V-man still clung to his grip on the gun. If Rahim managed to win, that would be the end. His hand felt slick where it held on. When V-man looked down, he saw the blood from his shoulder had soaked down through his shirt and was dripping down toward the handle of the gun. Inch by inch, the gun slipped from his hand until he no longer felt it in his fingertips. A moment later, Rahim turned the gun around, and V-man was looking straight down the barrel.

V-man threw himself backward in the hopes that the shot would miss. The gunfire was deafening. He quickly looked over his body for a wound but realized that aside from his shoulder and some pretty serious bruises, he was still intact. In front of him, Rahim swung around furiously, trying to dislodge the young woman from his back. Anna's blonde hair flew wildly, making it hard to see either one of them.

With a wild scream, she sank her teeth into Rahim's arm. The gun went flying before it skidded across the ground with a metallic scraping sound. V-man lunged for the gun, turned and aimed. The only problem was the lack of clear target.

"Anna, get out of the way!" V-man shouted.

"Thanks for the tip!" she said. Clearly, the request was easier said than done. If Anna let go while Rahim moved so erratically, she would go flying. They also ran the risk of him running or grabbing her as a human shield. She must have weighed these possibilities and decided the safest place was to remain clinging to his back. That didn't advance their cause, though, and V-man was left holding his gun at the ready, waiting for a shot.

Rahim reached across his body. A glint reflected off his hand, shining in V-man's eyes. By the time he realized what was creating the reflection, it was too late.

"No!" he yelled.

At the same time, Anna screamed in pain. Rahim drew the knife across her arm, and she fell from him. He turned, lifting the knife to plunge it into her chest, but V-man finally had the shot he needed. He took it. The body shot knocked the terrorist to the ground. He was mortally wounded but still conscious.

V-man, looking down at the terrorist, pressed the gun to Rahim's forehead. His breath came in shallow gasps.

Dying, Rahim's looked up at V-man. He looked past the 9mm and read the four words under the tattoo on V-mans arm. . The Real American hesitated a moment, staring directly at Rahim, and that slight grin came upon his face. Slowly he pulled his 9mm slightly back and shot the terrorist in the middle of his forehead.

At some point after the shooting, AC had joined them and was now looking over V-man's shoulder at the dead man. Rahim's eyes had glazed over, staring into the sky.

"That means we still have to stop the bomb," V-man said. "Take care of Anna. And get these people out of here!"

"Who?" AC asked.

V-man motioned toward Anna, lying on the ground, cradling her arm. Then stood and raced toward the building. He came face to face with angry, beady eyes peering at him over the top of a black bandana. He shook his head and sighed. The guy held a baseball bat in his hand and was smacking it against his open palm, trying to appear threatening.

"I don't have time for this shit," V-man said.

"Now let's see who comes out on top," the boy said. Behind him, a group of ten or fifteen angry young men wearing black costumes stared at V-man. The kid lifted the bat, preparing to swing. When the bat came down, V-man's hand came up with lightning speed and twisted the bat up and to the side, putting the kid's wrist at too awkward of an angle to keep hold of the bat. Once V-man held the bat in his hands, he swung it hard. It landed with a crack, laying the leader, if he could be called that, out flat against the pavement. He would live, but he would remember V-man for a long time to come. The others weren't intimidated by the quick takedown of their leader. Instead they pressed forward as an angry, irrational mob. Before they could make it to V-man, two young men streaked through their number, throwing fists with powerful fury. Homer and Jerome had arrived (in more ways than one).

"We got this, V-man. Go do what you have to do," Jerome shouted. Soon, Big Mike, AC, and Jay joined the younger guys in pummeling the protesters. V-man couldn't imagine what they had to even protest, but it didn't matter. They were looking for trouble, and they found it. He had more important things to worry about. He left his friends to it and turned toward where he had last seen Jasim.

He pushed through the crowd to stop in front of the police tape and temporary orange fencing around the steps of the courthouse. The reporter cowered in a corner, still clutching her microphone and speaking into a camera. V-man gave her credit for bravery, but it was a pretty stupid choice. The stone steps made a V shape, leading up toward the door. Each step was at least a few feet wide, and where the steps met the wall, they held deep shadows as columns reached for the overhang that jutted out from the roof a few stories up.

Squinting against the juxtaposition of sun and shadows, V-man studied the partially hidden corners. Shadows tried to play tricks on his eyes. Each one looked like it had the potential to be hiding a young man. It wasn't until he saw the black strap of a book bag trailing out into a small streak of sunlight that he knew for certain. He looked around at the hundreds of people on the steps and in front of the building.

"Get out of here," he shouted to the reporter.

She looked up with renewed panic but didn't move.

"There is a bomb! Get out of here," V-man shouted again. Finally, the stubborn woman and her camera crew, along with the others who had been huddling near her, stood and began running. They picked up the alarm, warning others that there might be a bomb. It was the best he could do to protect them. When he looked back, the book bag strap was gone. He ran to the column where it had been sticking out, but no one was there. V-man's head turned quickly until he caught sight of Jasim retreating down the steps.

"Jasim!" he called.

Jasim paused to look back at V-man. Emotions passed so quickly across his face that V-man couldn't keep track of them. He thought he saw sadness or regret, but maybe that was wishful thinking because Jasim turned his back on him and kept jogging down the sidewalk.

Jasim stayed on V-man's side of the barricade, close to the wall. V-man ran to catch up. When he was a few steps behind, he reached out and grabbed hold of the backpack slung on his back.

"Let go," Jasim yelled.

Jasim slid out of the bag, letting it come away in V-man's hand and kept running as best he could through the crowd. V-man stopped to catch his breath while opening the bag. It felt too light to carry anything worthwhile. When he peered inside, his suspicions were confirmed. The bomb was on Jasim.

"Jasim, please talk to me! For Luca's sake," V-man yelled, raising his gun. Jasim was a few feet away. V-man's words gave him pause.

"Listen, Mr. Papavese, get out of here. Tell Luca I am sorry." His voice held unshed tears. He sounded younger than V-man knew he was. Jasim fished in his pocket and pulled out a black remote.

"Jasim. Don't do it." V-man's hand holding the gun shook as sweat dripped into his eyes. He should pull the trigger, but some part of him held onto the hope that the young boy his son had grown up with would somehow resurface and come to his senses. "You are a good boy. You don't have to do this. I don't know what Rahim filled your head with, but your life doesn't have to end here. What purpose does that serve? Rahim was using you to fulfill his own need for glory."

Jasim looked down at the detonator in his hand and looked back at V-man. Now V-man could see the tears in his eyes. A war raged behind his eyes. V-man couldn't tell which side was winning.

"Rahim is dead," V-man said. "So are his friends, but yours aren't. You aren't alone. Luca is worried about you."

Jasim's conflicted eyes watched V-man. The detonator seemed to be forgotten in his hand.

"Drop it!" The voice came from off to Jasim's right side.

V-man looked up, and Jasim's head turned toward the sound as he tightened his grip on the detonator. It was Chief Williams. He held a gun leveled on Jasim. Time came to a halt as V-man watched the chief pull the trigger. The bullet blasted from the barrel as the gun kicked back in his hand.

"No!" V-man screamed when he realized where the bullet was aimed. Jasim's head snapped backward, and blood coated the sidewalk and gray cement blocks behind him. He seemed to fall in slow motion as V-man watched helplessly. He landed with a thud, the detonator falling from his hand onto the sidewalk. V-man ran toward him before he realized what he was doing.

He knelt before the boy's body, picking up the lifeless form to cradle him in his lap. He seemed so small and fragile lying there. There was no life left in his eyes; they stared innocently toward the heavens. V-man felt tears threaten to spill from his eyes as he whispered, "It's okay now."

He hated himself for not being able to save the boy, a casualty of dangerous ideology and a need for self-importance. V-man knew Jasim hadn't been the young boy that his son had played with for the bulk of his life, but he couldn't be angry at Jasim. The boy deserved to live. He should have been able to save him the same way Amesh had saved Luca. Rahim had seen his vulnerability and played upon it until it became a deadly sickness.

CHAPTER EIGHTEEN

V-MAN DIDN'T KNOW HOW LONG HE KNELT ON THE
hard pavement of the sidewalk, holding Jasim's body. When he had been
Jasim's age, he had already completed a tour of Vietnam and was starting
his own business, but now, looking at the boy, who had grown up beside
his own son, it felt terribly too soon for him to die. Chief Williams stood
a few paces away, barking commands into his radio. Soon, an entire battalion of police officers dressed in full riot gear marched through the
street. Shortly after that, EMTs swarmed the area, but none of them
approached Jasim. That was followed by the bomb squad. Men dressed
in armor and faceplates surrounded V-man and with heavy hands pulled
him away from Jasim's body.

"You know him?" Chief Williams said as he walked V-man to the
perimeter that had been set up.

"Huh?" V-man said, becoming aware of the man walking alongside
him for the first time.

"The kid?" Chief Williams said again, pointing his thumb back
toward the bomb squad. "You know him?"

"Yes I do. " V-man said. "I know his father."

"Well, the Feds are going to be all over this. I am sure they are going
to want to talk to you."

"That's fine," V-man said. "Hey, listen, do me a favor. Let me tell the kid's dad."

Chief Williams thought about the request for a few minutes. V-man imagined he was going over the rules and regulations about notifying the next of kin. Finally, he nodded. "All right, but do it soon. Otherwise, I won't have a say in the matter."

"Thanks, Chief. I owe you one," V-man didn't stop at the safety perimeter. He kept walking. Soon he was joined by AC, Jay, big Mike, Homer, Jerome, and Anna. AC had an arm around Anna, who cradled her arm. V-man didn't bother walking to his car, and neither did anyone else. The police and emergency vehicles only added to the congestion. The EMTs tried to stop the wounded group, but V-man brushed them aside. They didn't move much faster than a crawl until they were three or four blocks away from the courthouse. News reporters tried shoving cameras and microphones in their faces to ask questions about how close they were to the action and what their reaction to all of it was, but they were rudely dismissed by curses and shoved by more than one person in the huddled group.

When they pushed open the doors to the bar, a worried Brenda looked up from her position on the floor where she had been scrubbing on hands and knees.

"Oh, thank God!" she said, her Irish accent thicker with her worry. "I was watching the news, and I just couldn't take it anymore. I had to keep myself busy." She stood up and wiped her hands on her apron that had turned a dirty brown from crawling around on the floor.

No one had escaped the courthouse unscathed. Brenda hustled behind the bar, coming back out with clean rags, buckets of water and alcohol.

The adrenaline that had been keeping V-man on his feet during the fighting despite the gunshot wound had slowly seeped away during their long walk back. His body sank into the first chair he saw. The others did the same.

"Everyone find a seat," Brenda said, passing out the clean white rags. "First we need to stop the bleeding."

"Shouldn't we just go to the hospital?" Jerome asked.

Everyone stared at him as if he had committed heresy.

"When we are ready," V-man said.

Jerome shook his head, essentially saying, "Suit yourself." Jerome and Homer had some pretty bad scrapes and cuts, but nothing compared to the rest of the group, so Jerome grabbed an extra towel from the stack next to Brenda. "Who's first?" he said.

"Help Anna," V-man said. "Apply some pressure to that wound. She may need stitches, but we won't know 'til it is cleaned up."

Jerome did as he was told. Homer picked up an extra towel and stepped up beside him next to Anna. Jerome studied him from out of the corner of his eye. Hey, "Homie."

"Thanks for the help out there," Jerome finally said, turning his attention to the seeping wound on Anna's side. Homer nodded and smiled. The two big men shared a quick glance.

Brenda went to V-man first.

"Don't fuss over me," V-man said irritably.

"Don't be ridiculous. You have the most severe wound. Now sit down and stop your whining," Brenda said as she pressed a wet cloth firmly against his shoulder. He sucked in a startled breath at the sting before glaring at her. The glare didn't last long. The door to the bar opened. V-man stood up abruptly when he saw who was on the other side.

"Sit back down," Brenda grumbled. She had never seen the men standing in the doorway before, so she didn't understand V-man's and Jays excited reaction.

"LaBamba," V-man said. He and Jay rushed forward toward the man in the wheelchair. Behind him followed the now familiar group of young men who had originally greeted him in little Mexico. V-man nodded at Gomez, who in turn did the same.

"How did I know you would need me to save your ass again?" Valenzuela said. His thick Spanish accent hadn't changed since V-man had last spoken to him over forty-five years ago.

"Sure as hell glad you did." V-man wrapped his arms around Valenzuela's shoulders. He hadn't been expecting the hug, but eventually reached his arms up and hugged V-man back. "It's been too damn long."

Valenzuela nodded. "It's been a hard journey for me. I took a long time accepting my altered physical state. Learning to depend on others nearly killed me. No one wanted to give me a job. Everywhere I went, and everything I did was a constant and brutal reminder of my disability. I fell into a serious depression for many years. I almost didn't make it out of it. Not thinking about the war was the only thing that kept me sane. That included the people that had been there."

The others had suffered some bruising, cuts, and scrapes, but nothing that posed a threat to their lives. They worked on cleaning their own wounds. No one spoke. The sound of water gently splashing, and the occasional grunt of pain broke through the silence every so often. Brenda wore a look of concern but knew better than to push for explanations before V-man was ready.

"Every time I close my eyes, I watch that boy die again and again," V-man finally said.

Sad, sympathetic eyes turned to him.

"It wasn't your fault," Anna finally responded.

Thank you, Anna. I know what happened. I know I just have to live with it," V-man said. His tone was gentle but sad.

"He lost his way. It would have been great if we could have brought him back, but we couldn't. You and I and everyone in this room made the choice to put our responsibility to this country and everything it stands for above all else, including our own safety. If it had been a choice between letting him blow himself up on some jihad mission or killing him, you would have pulled the trigger yourself. Once he made that decision to strap a bomb to himself, he was no longer ours to protect."

V-man nodded. He had found a kindred spirit in Anna. With everyone in the room, in fact. They were all real Americans.

Every head in the place turned toward the door when it slammed open. At one point or another, Brenda had turned the sign that hung on the door from "open" to "closed," so no stragglers walked into the make-shift infirmary. That didn't stop the uniformed officers from barging in. No one spoke for what felt like a full minute.

"All right, what do you want?" V-man finally said. The pain in his shoulder had only gotten worse as Brenda had rubbed it with alcohol. He had no patience left. We are Detroit PD.

We have been informed people here were involved in a shooting today. We will need to interview everyone.

Anna reached into a pocket and pulled out her badge. "Homeland Security," she said curtly." We have priority here, and I am investigating this as an act of terrorism. "

There was a momentary standoff.

Then Chief Williams stood in the doorway. Everyone just paused.

Chief Williams walked slowly in, taking in the sight of everyone's partially bandaged wounds. "I would have been here sooner, but I got tied up with the Feds.

Looking at the Detroit PD contingent, he said, "I got this. Nobody here was involved. Meet me back at Headquarters.

"He looked at AC, meeting his eyes. They held gratitude that V-man had never seen before.

He turned and started walking out. The rest of his unit stood frozen in disbelief.

"I said, "Let's go."

They all followed him out.

CHAPTER NINETEEN

AFTER DOING WHAT THEY COULD AT THE BAR AFTER the fight, Brenda had eventually convinced him to head to the hospital to get professional help. The nurses had held him far longer than he thought was necessary after cleaning the wound and sewing him up. Jethro, Big Angel, Mad Dog, and Dragon Lady, along with KBoy, had arrived at the hospital to check on the V-man. He felt like shit. He hadn't slept the night before, and he felt every bruise, cut, and bullet wound on his body. But upon seeing his biker brothers and sisters, it was quite clear, to him, his ride had arrived. He immediately dressed, and with little resistance from the nurses, the six of them headed to the Corner Bar. KBoy was honored as V-man jumped on the back of his chopper and winked at him and gave him a high five, and they sped away. It was just what the doctor had ordered. He was energized. As they entered the bar, V-man could not describe the feelings he had for all who were there. They were his people, bound by the common thread of love for country and for another and willing to sacrifice at any costs and defend this country from all enemies foreign or domestic. When he needed them they were there. They were the Real Americans.

"Shouldn't you be laid up somewhere, nursing your wounds?" AC asked.

"The best remedy for me right now is to be right here. " V-man said. "That hospital is awful; they wake you up every goddamn hour to check your blood pressure. Although, even if they had let me sleep, I doubt I could have. Been thinking about Amesh."

"Yeah, man. I have been keeping an eye on the news. They haven't released names yet, but I am sure the guy will put it together. You tell him what happened yet?"

"No, I told him to meet me here. He should be here soon," V-man said, glancing at the clock.

After V-man had a cold beer in his hand, but before he could take the first sip, Amesh walked through the front door like a hurricane of anxiety. A normally well-put-together man, he stood before V-man completely disheveled. His hair was uncombed, and his shirt was untucked.

"Please, tell me what has happened?" Amesh pleaded, grabbing onto V-man's good shoulder. "I know it is terrible. I have been watching the news, but I just . . . I have to know . . . What happened? Where is Jasim? Do the police have him in custody? Did he hurt anyone?"

V-man closed his eyes and took a deep breath before looking Amesh in the eyes. "I am sorry, my friend. Jasim is dead."

All of the life drained from Amesh's face as his muscles went slack. Amesh fell backward into the stool behind him. "No," was all he said. "But . . . no."

"He didn't hurt anyone. He was deeply confused,"

"Tell me how it happened," Amesh said.

A scraping sound and a gust of breeze announced another person coming into the bar. V-man looked up briefly to see Anna step inside. She walked stiffly but otherwise looked better than when he had last seen her the day before. V-man turned back to Amesh, who remained unaware of what was happening around him. After a moment's pause, V-man began telling the story of what happened to Jasim.

Anna waited on the opposite side of the long bar, acutely aware of the difficult conversation taking place in the far corner. The man sobbed openly, and V-man awkwardly patted him on the back, although she could tell he truly felt for the man he was comforting.

"I just . . ." he began before he was choked off by a sob. "I just wish that he wouldn't be remembered for this. His name will be all over the news soon. No one will believe that he was a good boy before all this."

"I do, and so do you. Everyone that knew Jasim understood the person he was before Rahim came," V-man said.

"It is all my fault. I should have seen it sooner. I should never have let that man into my home! You just never think. You never think your own son could get caught up in that. You always think it happens to other people, not you."

"What can I get you?" AC asked quietly, pulling Anna's attention back around.

"Oh, I will just have a coffee. I have a long drive back tonight." Anna had spent the night at a local hotel at V-man's insistence, after being checked out at the hospital.

"You got it," AC said. He poured the fragrant black liquid into a mug and handed it to her. "What brings you back?"

"I just wanted to say goodbye to everyone, and I wanted to thank V-man. He saved my life more times than I could count yesterday. I had been following that guy for weeks. Without V-man, I wouldn't have been able to catch him."

"Man, you don't need to thank V-man," AC said with a dismissive wave of his hand. "He lives for this!"

Anna laughed.

"No really. He sees it as his duty. He doesn't see things the way other people do. Most people, you know, they go about their lives, and when they see something that ain't right, they come up with a million excuses why it isn't their problem. Either they don't know the people, or they too busy, or whatever the reason. Somehow, no matter what it is, it ain't never their problem. V-man, well, he's the opposite. He looks for people in need. When he sees something going wrong, doesn't matter what it is, he comes up with reasons why it is his situation and then figures out how to fix it. He doesn't take any of this for granted. He knows what a privilege it is to be an American and have all the freedoms and liberties we got. V-man isn't going to let anyone mess with the good thing we got. That's what makes V-man so special. Make sense?"

"Strangely, it does," Anna said. She had the same feelings when she had joined Homeland Security, and when she first started following Rahim. While she sat waiting for V-man to finish his conversation, a man in a wheelchair, followed by some younger Hispanic guys, came in. She remembered V-man calling him LaBamba. After him, Jay joined them, followed by Big Mike from the back. They all hung around in their own private corners, keeping one eye on the V-man's conversation.

"Can I get you something?" Big Mike asked Valenzuela's group. Valenzuela looked suspiciously at the small menu before finally asking for one of each of the three dishes.

"Good choice," Mike said.

At the other end of the bar, Amesh stood up suddenly, knocking over the stool he had been sitting on.

"Amesh, why don't you stay here a little bit and calm down?" V-man said.

"No, no, I have to talk to Napor. She has been worried sick. I dread telling her," Amesh said.

"You want me to go with you?" V-man said.

"No, this is something I have to do. I will carry the burden of his death forever, and this is just one part of that."

"I don't like you going alone."

"Thank you, V-man. You have been a good friend to my family and me. Thank you for looking out for Jasim when I couldn't." With that he turned his back on V-man and walked out the door.

As soon as the door was closed, everyone in the bar moved to huddle closely around V-man, finding chairs to sit on or leaning up against the bar to stand, except AC. He grabbed his jacket and picked up a large manila-colored envelope.

"What you got there?" V-man asked.

"Just some unfinished business. Keep an eye on the bar," he said to no one in particular before he walked out.

The evening was settling on Detroit, and AC was worried he wouldn't catch the chief still at his desk, especially with the investigations that must be going on since yesterday, but he had to try. If he wasn't there, he would leave the envelope on his desk, and he would read it eventually. AC didn't know what he expected the chief to do with the information.

AC pushed through the doors of the police station. The receptionist looked up when he came in.

"I need to see Chief Williams, please," AC said, trying to be polite.

"What is this regarding?" she asked.

"It is private and urgent."

She picked up the phone and pushed an extension. "Hello, Chief, there is a man out here to see you. He said it is an urgent personal matter." She paused, listening, then looked up at AC. "What is your name?"

"AC," he said. She repeated his name back into the phone before hanging up.

"All right, the chief will see you. Third door on the left."

AC walked the short distance to the chief's office. The man sat behind his desk, looking like he hadn't slept in days.

AC dropped the envelope on the desk without saying a word while he held the chief's gaze. The chief's hard eyes studied AC before dropping down to the envelope.

"What's this?" he asked, pulling the envelope toward him.

"Just open it. It's information I thought you might want to know," AC said.

The chief opened the envelope and pulled out the small stack of papers that had been stored inside. His brow creased with confusion as he looked at the documents before understanding and shock lit up his face.

"Jerome?" he said. His voice sounded weak and far away without any of his typical bombastic nature. "He's mine?"

AC turned and left the chief to puzzle through the new connection they had. He imagined he would be hearing from him again very soon.

AC got back to the bar to see the diverse group of friends had finally started relaxing as they threw back a few beers. He found his usual spot behind the bar, making sure the beers kept coming. Each one had a vastly different background that led them to sit in these seats with these people on this day, but the one thing they all had in common was a love for their country and a need to protect it at all costs. That bond would hold them together for as long as they lived.

"V-man," Anna said. "I just wanted to say thank you. You didn't have to step in, but you did, and you saved my life, along with everyone else at that courthouse yesterday."

V-man looked at the young proud Border Patrol Agent. She had been stellar under fire and maintained her cool in a high-pressure situation. She was tough. She was brave and dedicated. "I am proud to know you Anna. If you are a representation of your generation, I have faith in the future of our country. It would be an honor to meet your father and brothers and their friends. They answered the call when their country needed them. They are Real Americans, just like you and all the people here." Anna smiled softly at the V-man and turned to leave. She walked a few steps, stopped, turned and said, "You are the most amazing person I have ever met. I think you could teach General Patton a few things!" which drew a big smile from all. With that she walked out, anxious to get home. .

The rest of the group quietly sipped their drinks, enjoying sharing the space with trusted friends. They were family, brothers and sisters, patriots, keepers of their country, thinking about what they had been through together the day before.

"You know," V-man said, breaking the silence. "There is some trouble down in the Southwest with all that border stuff . . ." V-man let his thought trail off. All concerned and worried eyes turned to look at him. "Maybe time for a road trip!"

As he began to walk away, looking back he thought , "Never forget who we are, and never forget what it is that we do. We are the Americans, and we will go anywhere, anytime, and defeat any foe."

About the Author

Vito was born and raised on the east side of Detroit and entered the US Army in December 1965, Basic Training, Ft Knox, Kentucky; Advanced Infantry Training, Ft. Gordon, Georgia; Airborne jump School, Ft Benning, Georgia. Arrived in Vietnam in June 1966 as Airborne Infantry and volunteered to be Door Gunner on Assault Helicopters with First Air Cavalry, and was awarded the Distinguished Flying Cross and Air Medal with 18 Oak Leaf Clusters leaving in June of 1967. He rode motorcycles on the streets of Detroit for many years and with fellow bikers held some of the most successful fundraisers annually, attracting over 3000 supporters and raising $100,000.00s for various causes, including Children's Miracle Network, Michigan Vietnam Memorial, and Warren Police Department Benevolent Fund. In 2004, Vito began working with our retuning wounded Veterans and their families at Walter Reed. To date, have raised over $2,000,000.00 in helping families transition into civil life, in addition to sponsoring over 25 Guardian Angel Medical Service Dogs. In 2010 he was Builder of the Year for Homes For Our Troops. Since 2004, he has hosted his annual "Uncle Vito" Christmas Parties at Walter Reed and Ft Belvoir, VA. He has entertained over 5000 patients plus the families, caregivers, and children. He servers on the Board of Directors of the Yellow Ribbon

Fund which supports and helps severely wounded patients and their families transition into civilian life.

Awarded the National Good Neighbor Award in 2011 from the National Association of Realtors.

Awarded Commanders Award for Public Service by United States Army. For the past 11 years he has served on the Colorado Technical University Patriot Scholarship Committee which has awarded over 550 scholarships to veterans, caregivers and their dependents, valued at over $12,000,000.00.

A portion of the proceeds of the sale of this book will be donated to the Yellow Ribbon Fund and Guardian Angels Medical Service Dogs.

1st Cavalry Division 227 Assault Helicopter Battalion Vietnam 1966-1967

The Unspoken Bond Walter Reed National Military Medical Center

"Can't think of anyone better to entertain all of us while at the same time weaving in his personal insights. The reality is this Great Patriot is a man on a mission and he always gets the job done! Hopefully, the sequel will not be far behind."

AL GOLACINSKI
Retired Department of State Counter
Terrorism Specialist Hostage in Iran 1979-81